1 0 SEP 2012

IN THE RED

After twenty years as a bank clerk, Leslie Williams can stand the daily round no longer. He plans a crime—nothing very heinous, nothing more than a little dishonesty and a lot of unkindness. Yet, once he has made the first fatal move, he finds himself gathered into a fantastic web of adventure, mis-chance and danger.

The story takes place in London; the seedy hotel in Cromwell Road and the open-air market where he finds work as a salesman, are vividly seen through the eyes of Leslie Williams. He is a man who has broken loose, who doesn't know quite what dangers are hunting him from the past, or what sort of sense can be made of the present or future.

IN THE RED

Joan Fleming

First published 1961
by
Collins

This edition 2002 by Chivers Press
published by arrangement with
P. S. Field

ISBN 0 7540 8606 2

Copyright © 1961 by P. S. Field

British Library Cataloguing in Publication Data available

WIRRAL LIBRARY SERVICES	
5-9926920	
H J	947871
	£15.99
Cc	

Printed and bound in Great Britain by
Bookcraft, Midsomer Norton, Somerset

PART ONE

Mr. Leslie Williams

CHAPTER I

IT WAS lunch hour in the City. The large clock at the far end of the marble hall, situated grandly between two Ionic pillars, said three minutes to one. The bank was always crowded at lunch time but even bank cashiers must eat to live and the arrangement was that two out of the six cashiers would be away at a time.

The cashier in the fourth position from the door gave a particularly vigorous stamp to the last paying-in book he intended to deal with, pushed it briskly back to its owner, put up the small plastic disc announcing that the position was closed, and hurried off between the desks to the staff exit.

The cashier next to the door glanced quickly over his shoulder at the clock. Shaking his head slightly at the next customer, he reached for his " Till Closed " notice and put it down firmly in front of the small plaque which announced him as " Mr. Leslie Williams." With a look of annoyance, the next customer, and the three crowding upon his heels, shuffled up towards the adjoining position. Mr. Leslie Williams fixed his ball-point pen in its usual place in his waistcoat pocket, whisked the rubber stamp and a stray piece of blotting paper into the drawer, extracted twenty five-pound notes from the drawer, put them in the breast pocket of his jacket, stood up, pushed the stool tidily into place and walked out.

Whilst performing these simple movements he looked neither to left nor to right. He did not look to see whether the cashier to his left was observing him, nor any of the staff behind him in the body of the marble hall. He did not, in fact, care if anyone was observing him. He had gone through these movements in his mind so often for such a long time that he now acted purely automatically, watching himself with a slightly cynical sneer.

If anyone had seen him, he would have been saved: " Look what you're doing, old boy! " " Oh, ha ha! Be robbing the bank next! So absent-minded I must get myself seen to, eh? " Or if anyone had taken it seriously, there was always the " black-out " gimmick: " Had no idea what he was up to . . . been overdoing it . . . late nights . . . needs a holiday . . . slight breakdown."

But the simple fact was that nobody did see him, or if they did, refused to give credit to what they saw. A trusted employee of the City and Suburban Bank did not put a bundle of one hundred pounds into his pocket before going out to lunch. It did not happen, could not happen and anyone seeing it happen would know for certain that it had not happened, and that whatever they thought they had seen belonged to the realms of last night's dreams.

He had not intended to waste time going to the washrooms but sheer necessity drove him there. Then he unhooked his light plastic mackintosh from its peg and walked out into the fresh April air.

The other cashier whose lunch hour it was, was standing irresolutely on the edge of the pavement; he seemed to be sniffing the air with some delight and said, with unaccustomed cordiality: " Spring, Williams! Where are you off to? "

It was a stupid question; where would he be off to other than the usual lunch cafeteria? But Williams was a literal-minded man and the words: *I'm off to Paris on the four o'clock plane* were only restrained behind the barrier of his teeth at the cost of a grimace.

" The usual," he managed to say indistinctly.

" Come to the White Hart! "

But he hurried westwards towards the tube station and did not look back to see what impression he had made. Once he had attained the station, he felt more comfortable; in all the years he had travelled between the bank and Ealing Broadway, he had never met anyone he knew even by sight. He had travelled with thousands and thousands, even millions of people whom he had never seen before and whom he would never see again. To travel eternally on the London tube would be one way of being certain of avoiding detection, except, of course, that it closed for a few hours each night. Underground, the faces of one's fellow-travellers assumed a singularly apathetic expression; to enter the tube was like climbing on to the chimney piece and through the looking-glass; nothing, once that operation was performed, was quite the same on the other side. Perhaps he should travel as far as Ealing Broadway and back, again and again, and for ever, so that he would never have to face up to reality.

An empty stomach, that was what was wrong. In the carefully worked-out timetable, he had made allowance for a quarter of an hour in the public house near the station at Ealing; time for a glass of stout and a ham sandwich before taking a train to the air terminal. But first he had to go to his flat, in the modern block behind the Broadway, and pick up his suitcase which he had left ready.

If he had had any sense, he meditated, he would have brought out the suitcase with him on his way to work, and deposited it at a left-luggage office. He had, in fact, toyed with the idea but the main thing against doing so had been that at neither of the tube stations was there an official left luggage office and to ask the booking clerk to look after his case whilst he was at the bank would have been to draw unnecessary attention to himself.

So far, up to the moment when he was sitting in the tube on his way back home, everything had gone as to schedule; even the frightful scene with Lil. . . .

He had set the alarm clock to go off half an hour earlier that morning and had leapt from his bed before it stopped ringing. As usual he had made tea and brought a cup to Lil's bedside but this time he had woken her and told her to drink it up quickly. He himself drank two cups of tea in the kitchenette. Lil had called to him: " Half an hour too soon, Leslie. You are mean! "

He hurried purposefully back into the bedroom. For some months now he had been on the coolest of terms with his wife, saying nothing other than the remarks necessary for everyday life. Lil would be saying to herself, and to her friends, that he was " in a mood," and she wore that martyred air, yet faintly amused expression, which she always wore when such a state of affairs, call it what you like, existed. For a very long time he had been turning over in his mind, and aloud when alone in the flat, a whole lot of suitable phrases; fine rolling prose, some of them were. Others were mere clichés. When the time came, these phrases deserted him, like the remedial actions that a motorist plans in the event of a skid and which, when the skid occurs, escape him.

What he said was: " Lil, I have decided to leave you." And after a slight pause: " I am now thirty-eight, and so are you, and for fifteen years we have simply lived together out of habit. Life——"

But she had interrupted and said: " Oh my God! Les! You haven't felt like that all our married life. For heaven's sake! "

" Life——" he persisted, " is passing us by."

" Oh my God! " she cried. He knew he sounded like something out of *Women Only* but it was the sort of thing she could understand.

" So I am going to leave you——"

" To seek your fortune! You silly old fool! You can't do without me. You couldn't possibly get on without me now, after all these years."

She was wearing a rather pretty pink nightdress, a new one, he thought. And now she was pressing her hands to her breast in a rather appealing manner. He looked at the ceiling. " I bore you to death, and, frankly, you bore me. You won't suffer, Lil. You can more than look after yourself. You earn more than I . . . you can keep on this flat easily, and . . . have a good time, which is what you've always wanted, isn't it? "

Things weren't going quite the way he had planned.

Then he remembered one of the better phrases. " Life isn't meant to be simply *endured*, day after day, the same endless same old thing. Many better men than I have seen the light and have done this very thing that I am doing."

" Very thing . . . very thing," Lil repeated, bewildered.

He looked quickly at his expensive wrist watch, a present from Lil. Half of the half-hour he had allotted for this scene was nearly gone.

"Fortunately we have no children to consider——" He had not meant to say anything about children; that was Lil's Achilles' heel and he had not intended to strike his wife where it hurt most. He snatched up his suit where it hung ready, over the back of the chair, with the trousers across the seat, and took them into the bathroom where he shaved, washed and dressed. He went into the kitchen, made himself coffee and toast which he ate and drank standing by the gas stove. Having plenty of time in hand, he washed his cup, saucer and plate, as usual, and left them in the draining rack. He returned to the bedroom. She had plainly been crying heavily.

"Then you do mean it," she cried, "I can see from the expression on your face! Now will you let me say something?"

He glanced pointedly at his wrist watch and said patiently: "Go on, then."

"Listen, love, I believe in our marriage, I believe we've got something for each other, even if we haven't had any children. It may be a poor useless thing but I do love you in a way, Les. I do, in my fashion. I can't help being the sort of person I am, busy and flashy and over-efficient, and so on. But I was the same sort of person when you married me, and you loved me then."

"Oh, no you weren't. You were a very different person then."

"I *wasn't*——" She banged a fist silently on the bedclothes. "I was the same."

"You weren't!" It was absurd: I was ... you weren't ... was ... not ... was ... not ... like a couple of silly school kids. He thought: this isn't hurting me a bit, it is only making me feel we are being stupid. So if I am not being hurt, then she can't be. We're playing at feeling things, he thought.

"Don't go, Les. Let's start again. Let's try very hard this time, and I really mean *try*."

He shook his head. " It's no good. We've done it before . . . it never works out."

" When are you going? "

He could say: In God's good time, like his mother used to say, to tease him. Or he could say: now! He said: " As soon as I can possibly arrange it." She was in no state to say " Good-bye." At any moment she might become hysterical. He left the room, shutting the door gently behind him, and then the flat door, with equal care not to slam it.

And that was that. Lil had a job as supervisor in a West End coffee bar which served light meals and gaudy pastries. She left home as a rule at ten and returned after six; there was no chance of her being there when he came back at lunch time for his suitcase.

He had gone over every word that had passed between them several times before the train drew into Ealing Broadway station. Now he checked his watch with the station clock. The bus left the air terminal for the airport at ten to three. He ought to be back at his desk at the City and Suburban Bank at two exactly. If he had not appeared by half past two, they would have sent one of the upper clerks to take his place at the counter. The manager would have been told that he was not back from lunch and later on someone would be sent to his home to make inquiries as to whether he had been taken suddenly ill. Later . . . not quite yet. Not until close of business, at five o'clock, would his disappearance be taken seriously, when the hundred pounds was missed. And by that time he would be in the sky. By the time they had sent to his home and found no one there, had interviewed Lil later, had discussed the amazing facts and come to the unbelievable conclusion that Leslie Williams had really robbed the bank, embezzling one hundred pounds and decamped, he would be in Paris, as anonymous as one ant in a colony of ants.

He had found the small, tall, narrow hotel in the Place Dauphine when mooching about by himself in the Pont Neuf district on one of those occasions when Lil was giggling away with her friends on a sight-seeing tour round Montmartre, ending with a strip-tease cabaret; or going to the top of the Eiffel Tower. A small shabby hotel with its stucco chipping off badly, it faced the tiny square with its shady trees and strutting pigeons on one side and overlooked the river, seen through a lace of the green leaves of the plane trees, on the other. A few doors along was one of those restaurants with marble-topped tables and heavy-bosomed motherly waitresses who would kindly point out the most succulent items on the bewilderingly long menu.

He had written to book a room at this small hotel, heading the letter simply " London " and signing himself " Leslie W. Dunright (Mr.)."

Standing beside the counter in the pub near the station, he tore at his ham sandwich with the tough doughy crust and thought of the crisp French bread which he would soon break and plaster liberally with butter whilst waiting for the chosen dish. He drank the icy-cold foaming stout and thought of the carafe of *ordinaire* with which he would be left after he had finished the meal, and how he would sit on, for hours perhaps, drinking the red wine and feeling himself a man of the world, a man, at last, whom life was not passing by. Mr. Leslie W. Dunright.

He emptied the tankard of stout. And after a fortnight or so of leisure he would begin to see about things. A courier for a firm of holiday tours was what really appealed. Promoters of holiday tours were always ready to employ couriers; he was not bad looking, he had a certain amount of charm when he liked, and efficiency. Even without an additional language he could manage. He had integrity, anybody could see that at a glance. Integrity was what mattered in a job like that. No, there would be no difficulty in that direction. In fact, he would be able to pick and choose. He would, for instance, much prefer to direct a coach-load through the wine and olive belt, the warm countries round the Mediterranean, than, say, the northern capitals. The Holy Land, even, would offer no difficulties to him, versed, as he was, in all the more familiar Bible stories. If he were to spend not more than twenty-five pounds a week in Paris and started seriously to look for a job at the end of two weeks, he would still have money in hand to give him time to look round. And April was just the right time, when tours were being arranged and could not start without their couriers. Yes, he had thought of everything, every blessed little detail. It was this careful planning that left him so carefree now.

He was having a little trouble with his face; he felt self-conscious and his features were like ornaments on a chimney-piece which he could not quite arrange to his satisfaction. It was difficult to assume a look of bland normality with his mind an excited turmoil and the flesh of his face as stiff and unfamiliar as papier mâché. As he approached his home, he saw a group of tinies with whom he always exchanged a pleasantry, playing on the patch of grass in front of the flats with a tricycle and a mobile packing case. They were all under-fives who were not at nursery-school.

" Hi! " he hailed them with raised hand but somehow or other that was as far as he could get. He plunged into the entrance hall and up the concrete steps to the first floor with a burning flush staining these same unbiddable features.

As he took his key from his pocket, he reminded himself that he must leave it behind, in a conspicuous place. He must also, he reminded himself, once again, leave his cheque book and his National Health card, which he always carried about with him. He patted the pocket in which they now rested, together with his passport, the money he had taken from the bank, and the cash allowance with which he was allowed to leave the country.

As soon as his front door was opened, he was aware of a slight, a very slight unfamiliar and rather unpleasant smell. He went straight to the luggage cupboard where the expensive air-travel cases which Lil had bought for their foreign holidays stood carefully covered with a dust sheet. Underneath the sheet, his own case was already packed and contained his best black town suit and white satin tie, a sports jacket and light trousers, change of underwear, the gay shirt he had bought in Majorca to be worn outside the trousers and the dark brown suède shoes in real doeskin. These shoes had been bought secretly, without Lil's knowledge, at a small shop in Jermyn Street and had cost a very great deal of money, so much, in fact, that Leslie had known, when he bought them, that he had indeed crossed the Rubicon, that he would never be quite the same person again and that he had embarked upon a new way of life.

He slid out the case, uninitialled and, though full, still pleasantly light to carry. He opened the lid and put his plastic mackintosh inside. What about his umbrella? He wouldn't need it, of course, in the wine and olive belt but he would certainly need it in Paris where it could rain " cats and dogs." " Cats and dogs," he muttered whimsically as he went to fetch it from where it hung on its hook in the built-in cupboard in the bedroom.

He had certainly drawn back the curtains when he brought in Lil's early morning tea. Why, then, were they again drawn closely? He turned on the light. The switch beside the door operated only the wall plugs because Lil had great ideas about lighting and found a centre light " very unbecoming " in a bedroom. The two bedside lamps worked from a plug between the two beds and the dressing table lamp from another between the windows. All these had been switched off. He went over to the dressing table and turned on the small lamp. Lil was still in bed, but not as he had left her. She was lying partly over the side of the bed, and in the small space between the two beds, on the little white bedside rug, was a basin containing vomit. Her shoulders, barely concealed by the glamorous new nightie, were uncovered and her hair was hanging over her face in a most abandoned way.

Instinctively he moved forward and took hold of her shoulders to pull her back on to the pillows but as his warm hands touched her cold skin he gave a loud exclamation. He pulled her partially back on to her pillows and then snatched a looking-glass from the dressing table. With shaking hand, he tried to hold it to her nose and mouth, then took it across to the light to see if there was any condensation on the glass. Three times he tried the experiment but each time there was nothing on the glass. Frantically he seized her limp wrist and felt for her pulse; he could feel no movement at all. He peered into her livid face. Lil was always pale but now she was ashy, and blue round the lips.

" Oh, God! " He went across to the window to draw back the curtains in order to get a better light but stopped. Of course he must not do anything so foolish. Anybody outside might see him, there at his window, at a time when he was always in the City. He turned back to the bed and the bedside table, fumbling about amongst the pots of face cream, dirty cup and saucer, tumbler half full of water and found what he was looking for, the small brown bottle of pink sleeping tablets that they had kept ever since Leslie had pleurisy and the doctor had prescribed the tablets to give him good nights' sleep in spite of the awful pain which he suffered between his ribs. That tiny bottle had been in the table drawer, unused for at least four years. Pink pills, round and flattish, not like these new-fangled torpedo-shaped objects in violent colour which he knew many people took nightly. Harmless-looking small pink pills. However many had she taken? He poured the remainder into his palm . . . fourteen. How many had there been? She had taken them hurriedly because she had not even screwed the top back on the bottle. Had she gone on taking them one after the other until she became unconscious? He glanced again at her face, so utterly unlike Lil and quickly drew up the bedclothes and pulled the sheet right up over her head so that he could no longer see it.

He stood in the middle of the room, running his hands across his own face. This was a situation he knew all about. He had often read in who-dun-its about husbands in the same kind of predicament and each time he had thought impatiently how stupid the husband was. Why did these innocent husbands never, never get in touch at once with the police? That was what any normal, well-balanced, sensible man would do, without a moment's hesitation, because, if a man is not guilty of harming his wife, the simple fact will always stand out and the husband has nothing to fear. He had read of husbands going to infinite trouble to remove or conceal the body of their wives, though they were themselves perfectly innocent. He could almost write the hackneyed plot himself . . . " *Lil was quite, quite dead. What was he to do ?* "

Ring up the police at once, immediately and upon the instant.

He knew what he was going to do, though he didn't put it into thoughts yet. First, he had to go into the kitchen and find the rarely used bottle of rum and pour himself out a good stiff one, with a splash of water from the tap before he could reveal his actions to himself. He left the bedroom, turning off the light and closing the door gently.

Time was still well under control. He washed the tumbler from which he drank the rum, dried it and put it away. He noticed that the kitchen was as he had left it, there was no evidence of Lil having got herself any breakfast. He would slip out with his case and there would be no sign whatever that he had returned at all. No one would be likely to know how many travel cases they had, or what clothes he had taken. Under the circumstances it would be better not to leave the cheque book and the other evidence of his identity in the flat, this might look a bit out of the ordinary.

And then he shuddered violently. The telephone in the hall was ringing. That could be . . . someone from the coffee bar where Lil worked . . . or one of Lil's many friends. No, it wouldn't be a friend because everyone knew that Lil was out during the day on a week-day. Nor could it yet be the bank, it was only just on two o'clock now. It could be Lil's mother but she, too, would hardly be likely to ring now. Sheer agonising curiosity forced him towards the instrument but, as he put out his hand to raise the receiver, the ringing stopped.

It was time to go. He had planned to get a taxi to Cromwell Road air terminal but under the circumstances it would be better to take the train again. He shut the flat door quietly and ran downstairs, carrying the suitcase and breath-whistling to show how normal he felt. The children were still playing but any arrival or departure was of interest; they stopped for a moment to say " Hallo." It was absurd to think that any child of nearly five would not be quite capable of saying: " Oh, yes, I saw Mr. Williams coming out at dinner time . . . he was going away. He was carrying a case, like this."

So when he arrived at the air terminal he knew that he would not be leaving for Paris. It would not be accurate to say he realised it suddenly. He didn't. He had known it when he crossed the grass in front of his home and the children stopped to say " Hallo." It was only the rum he had drunk which helped him not to think, so that he continued to carry out the movements of his original plan.

The bus which was to take him to the airport would probably contain only a dozen or so passengers; the conductor would remember him easily. Then at the airport his seat on the Viscount was booked in the name of Mr. Leslie Williams; it was the last time he had intended to use his name but he had to do so because his passport was made out in that name and, though embarked upon a career of crime, he had not yet learned how to obtain a forged or faked passport. The arrival of Mr. Leslie Williams in Paris would be checked at Orly, but there he knew he would disappear satisfactorily enough to satisfy any police inquiries there might be about the Mr. Williams who had absconded with a hundred pounds.

Not, however, the Mr. Leslie Williams, wife poisoner. If the newspapers happened to be short of news and there was, in fact, very little happening at the moment, they might choose to make a big splash of the affair in the Ealing flat. His photograph might appear and the air hostess would easily be able to recognise the single man who travelled on that April day amongst the thirty or so passengers she would have in her care.

He went along to the wash-room and had a long careful look at himself in the looking glass, when he had the place to himself. He was five feet six inches in height, of medium weight with light brown hair, light brown eyes, dark suit, pale blue nylon shirt, dark grey tie. He had no scar, birthmark, mole, naevus or wen of any kind. It occurred to him that he could **as** easily come into being as Mr. Leslie W. Dunright here in London as in Paris. The question of becoming a courier would have to be shelved for the moment but only until such time as he could get a new passport under the assumed name.

He sat on a seat in the waiting hall, with his hands hanging limply between his knees, his suitcase beside him, and watched the little group of passengers forming for Flight No. 890 to Paris. He waited until they had been shepherded out of sight. He walked across to the litter bin and, taking his air ticket out of his pocket he looked at it for a long time. Though it was now valueless, to drop it into the litter bin was, somehow, final and inexorable.

"Can I help you, sir?" an official asked.

He jumped perceptibly. "No . . . no thanks!" He put the ticket back in his pocket, picked up his case and hurried out of the station; but the case seemed to have become considerably heavier. His shoulders were hunched against the weight as he walked out into Cromwell Road.

CHAPTER II

AND NOW the shock he had sustained and the rum he had drunk combined to have a strange effect upon him. It was as though his mind divided, so that he was half within himself, trudging the pavement, and half some way above himself looking down at his small struggling self pityingly. The insignificant creature was acting without thought or reasoning. He was moving towards his destiny with deadly impulsion. If it was true that those of us who do not develop strong personalities of our own are a combination of qualities inherited from our forebears then Leslie Williams was a mere mechanical toy, wound up by his playful ancestors, jigging and jolting along until the spring unwound.

The first hotel he came to was called Hotel Alpine. From the enormous, overpowering portico with its huge Corinthian pillars, he peered through the glass of the doors and saw the receptionist standing in the hall. He went in. She was talking to a waitress and took no notice of him at all.

How often had his mother laughingly told him that one of his great-great-grandfathers had been hanged for sheep-stealing in the market place in Welshpool. It was one of the elements in the make-up of the character of this scoundrel (and he meant scoundrel) that was his undoing at the present time. He was not acting out of character, he was obeying factors long dormant in him.

The receptionist looked at him with dislike. " Did you want something? "

" A room."

" A what? "

He cleared his throat. " A room, please. For one night? "

With a look of consternation, even concern, that he should require anything so extraordinary, she held open the door and watched his retreat down the steps with interest.

There was an establishment of exactly the same kind next door. He tried there without success.

And fourteen more. Cromwell Road, clearly, was not for him. But as soon as he turned out of Cromwell Road luck came his way; a black cat crossed his path. But not in the normal manner; the cat did not purposefully cross the pavement in front of him; it shot through the air, describing a low parabola, landing on the road with a fearful squawk, executing a magically deft sideways somersault to right itself and disappearing so fast down a nearby mews that it rivalled a Walt Disney cartoon.

" Cruel! " he exclaimed, looking quickly to see from what projector the cat had been fired. A large man dressed in a navy blue uniform with much gold braid was in the act of returning into the hall of yet another hotel; as he looked back he saw the shocked face of Leslie Williams and laughed. " That cat's had it coming to her," he explained pleasantly, " 'orrible thief! " He looked, at first glance, like an admiral, but on second thoughts must be a hall porter rather unusually and splendidly arrayed. He had kind eyes and hair grew from his ears.

"You haven't a room available, I suppose?" Leslie asked wistfully.

" Yes, sir, we have, sir." The hall porter actually came down the steps and took the suitcase. But once inside the hall, he divulged that it was a double room. It had been booked for weeks for a young couple arriving by air from the East; the wife had been taken ill before departure and the telegram cancelling the room had arrived " not above an hour ago. So you're in luck, sir! "

A double room was not what he wanted, but never mind. Any room, any room in which he could be quiet and alone to think over the monstrous happenings of the last three hours would do.

The hall porter brought out the visitors' book and his manner was so friendly and personal that some quick improvisation had to be done. " Leslie W. Dunright, Louis XIV Hotel, Paris," he wrote, Louis XIV being the only French king he knew.

" And how long would you be staying, sir ? "

". A little uncertain. I have to get some business fixed up——"

" A week ? "

" About that. But I don't really want a double room, you know."

" Single rooms is very much in demand, sir, very much in demand. But if you leave it to me, sir, something might be arranged ... Sawley is the name. It's like this, we've got very little moving in and out, most of our people is residents, live 'ere all the year round. Oh, we've some very nice people, mostly elderly gentlefolk. This young couple whose room you're having had an old aunt lived here years and years, till she was carried off with a stroke. That's how they came to know of us."

" What is the name of this hotel ? "

" The Lugano, sir."

He wondered why so many of them carried Italian names with their faint reminder of sunshine and blue lakes and snow-covered mountains.

" Could you have some tea sent up to my room, Sawley ? "

" Very good, sir, I'll see to it."

Hard-boiled, that was what you would call Lil. Not the sort to commit suicide. Anybody would say that with the greatest conviction; self-confident, managing, cheerful, with any amount of friends. He could hear any one of them now giving evidence at the inquest; " Mrs. Williams was the very last person to commit suicide; she had no worries at all, if she had, she'd have told us about them; she was not one to hide anything. One of the nicest women I have ever known," he could hear her employer saying and retiring from the witness box in tears.

That Lil should empty a quarter of a bottle of sleeping tablets down her throat simply because her meek and colourless husband had told her he was about to leave her was not in character. She wouldn't deal with the situation that way. She would do something else: she would . . . for instance . . . she would be defiant, putting on her make-up extra carefully and stepping out in her best suit with her best bag tucked under her arm and a cheerful smile on her face to show that she didn't give a damn.

She would never, never, never get out of bed, draw the curtains, turn out the lights and poison herself.

And yet . . . that, precisely, is what she has done! he thought. A letter! Suppose she had left a note for him saying what she was going to do? He hadn't thought of that. But neither had he seen a note and, if anyone left a suicide note, they left it in a conspicuous place.

No, he must face it. If there was one thing Leslie could not stand in others and which, it seemed now he had in himself, in full measure, it was cruelty. Cruelty which probably stemmed from that self-same sheep-stealing ancestor. It was cruelty to say anything to her about children. Fourteen years ago the doctors had said they could see no reason at all why Lil could not have children and she had come home radiant, to bury her head in Leslie's shoulder and weep with joy.

And then nothing more had been said; week after week, month after month, year after year, nothing had been said but hope had faded and Lil had stayed cheerful and looked happy, but, inside, she had been getting harder and harder and more and more aloof. And now, this awful, unkind thrust he had given her this morning . . . was it only this morning? It must have been that, there was no other explanation that fitted at all, and even that didn't fit quite perfectly. In what mood did she take the tablets? Remorse? Anger? Sorrow? Despair?

So the answer was quite simple; though he had not killed her in actual fact, he had certainly killed her theoretically, which is almost as bad.

But the trouble was that he had brooded over, planned and dreamed about the way he was going to leave her for so long that the whole scheme had taken on a life and momentum of its own; when the time came *it couldn't be stopped.*

And, in the same way, he thought gloomily, an atom bomb would be dropped long after the desire to drop it had passed, simply because it had been made to be dropped, planned to be dropped . . . it finally would be dropped.

And that was why, when this morning, he at last took hold of the money at the bank and put it in his pocket, he had almost longed for someone to see him so that the whole frightful plan could be stopped.

Of course, it was not every plan that became imbued with that kinetic energy; lots of plans remained merely plans, but some plans were destined to live for a time and others to live until they reached fruition, when they exploded. As this plan had exploded.

And left a newly-born, rather colourless, very ordinary man of thirty-eight, with no talents, nor any outstanding qualities (not even integrity now), lying on a bed in a double bedroom which he could not afford, in a dismal hotel in South Kensington.

He didn't want any dinner but, if he were going to stay here for a while, the dining-room would have to be faced, sooner or later; he might as well face it now.

Sawley was now dressed in a white coat and was the waiter, assisted by an extremely young waitress. He was shown to a double table against the wall. Though the dinner gong had only just rung, and Leslie had hurried to be in the dining-room before the others, he found every table already occupied and noted that the residents of the Lugano made a point of punctuality for meals. There were only eight tables, four double and four single, accommodating twelve guests in all. Three elderly couples occupied the other double tables and the single tables were occupied by two ladies, neither middle-aged nor young, and two men, one of them so old that he was bent nearly double and shook perpetually and the other a bored-looking young foreigner who read the *New Statesman* throughout the meal.

The situation was ludicrous, he thought bitterly, yet terrible; he had been, and still was, possessed by fear. It was this that had stopped him from leaving the country which, he saw now, was probably what he should have done in spite of what had happened. If one is going to be a criminal, one must make up one's mind to be one, not a mere cringing, spineless thief. From now on, he thought, looking round sourly, he was going to shed the Demon Fear. After a good night's sleep, he hoped, the shock he had sustained to-day would have receded, leaving him free to develop his new self, Leslie W. Dunright, and to look back on his old self with no more emotion than he would show over a cast-off suit of clothes.

The next move must be to get rid of every evidence of his connection with Leslie Williams. His passport and chequebook and air ticket to Paris would have to be destroyed. He would apply for a new passport at once, and within a week, with luck, he should have it; without any bookings of air passages, he would simply go to Victoria, take the train to Dover, cross by boat and take the first train to Paris along with hundreds of other travellers. Soon, very soon now, he would be sitting on that seat in the Place Dauphine watching the pigeons strutting about at his feet. This day dream had been nurtured for so long that it had achieved the importance of the Holy Grail; the Place Dauphine image was the symbol of his future as a person as opposed to that of a nonentity and if it were not to be achieved he would have nothing more to live for; no interests, no hobby, no ambition; simply, as somebody whimsically put it: " Thames for one."

He became aware that from a table across the room, a woman was giving him animated looks which he was determined not to meet. Between looks, however, he allowed his glance to sweep over her and was able to decide that she was about his own age, well-dressed and with an abundance of fading reddish hair. Her manner was that of one who thinks herself considerably younger than she is. After a time, his teeth were set on edge by her behaviour as the fascinating young girl amongst the crowd of old fogies.

He gave his attention to the woman sitting at the tab'e next to her. She could be somewhere between forty and forty-five. She had a lot of thick brownish-silver hair which was drawn back from her face and piled up in a modern style, leaving the line of her jaw exposed. Though she was not pretty, Leslie stared at her in admiration; she looked dignified, neat and oddly attractive. Her small yellowish face was barricaded by a pair of huge horn-rimmed spectacles and she took no notice of anybody; she was reading a book as she ate.

He ate his own meal slowly so that he would not draw attention to himself by leaving the dining-room before the others. But he need not have bothered. People consumed their dinner hurriedly and there was a general scamper for the best chairs in the TV room. Several nodded pleasantly to him as they passed his table. Presently he and Sawley, the hall porter, acting waiter, were alone.

"There's coffee in the lounge, sir."

Leslie shook his head.

"Can't face them," Sawley observed. "Well, I don't blame you, sir. But they're a decent enough lot when you get used to them. Those three old couples have been here since long before I came; eight and ten years, so I believe. The manageress wouldn't have them go for anything!"

It appeared that Sawley was at present in charge of the whole place because the manageress, who lived in a flat at the top of the house, was away on her honeymoon in Australia. A number of people came in during the day, receptionist, waitress, cook, cleaners, but by eight o'clock at night they had all gone and Sawley was wholly responsible for locking up and seeing that all the lights were out.

"Bit of a tie, isn't it?"

"If I do want an evening out, the waitress stays till I'm home. I sleep in a room in the basement, next the kitchen, see? So if ever you want the odd cup of tea late, it's O.K. by me. I'm not out often, not much of a gadabout. None of us in this place is. They're not often out, except Miss Lino; she's our gay young spark but she's got her own key and lets herself in and out as she likes."

"Miss Lino!" Leslie smiled, "surely not!"

"That one!" Sawley indicated where the red-haired one had been sitting. "She's half French. Lived here years. She used to be here with her old father and when he died she stayed on. He left her a nice little bit of money so she's got her own car and she's often away. But she pays for her room all the same."

"But not *Lino!*"

"It's spelt like this," Sawley brought out the stub of a pencil and wrote laboriously on the back of the menu. "LYNEAUX, Lizzie Lino," he chuckled.

"And that one, sitting there?"

"Ah, that's Miss Brown. 'Erminey Brown; she's nice, that one. She keeps herself to herself, as you might say. A bit of what you'd call a dark horse, or a dark mare, eh?" Sawley gave a snort of laughter and then, talking about horses, launched out into a dissertation on the coming week-end's racing for, it seemed, he was a passionate punter. After listening for a long time Leslie primly remarked: "I'm afraid I never go to the races, it's just not one of my things."

"I don't go to the races neether," Sawley exclaimed robustly. "Horses . . . can't stand the sight of the b . . . . . . s. Stupid, that's what they are . . . temperamental like women. I've always kept off of women and horses."

"How can you say that?" Leslie asked mildly.

"I never see a bloomin' horse from one year's end to the other!"

"In that case," Leslie returned with the sweet reasonableness of the bank cashier he was, "why bet on horses? There are always dogs you could put your money on, or, if you didn't care for the dogs . . . there's the football pools!"

Sawley made a contemptuous sound: "Dogs! It's a real common lot you get dog racing. Common scum! I wouldn't go dog-racing not if you paid me. And as for football pools, there's no skill in it! Any old boozer can fill in those forms and get himself fixed up with a cool hundred. No brain required for that."

"I should have thought you required some ability to fill in football pool forms," Leslie returned, "I've often heard people say they were too complicated for them." And then Sawley told him that, though he, as he had said, never set eyes on a horse, he knew the history of every important piece of horse flesh in the stud book; it was breeding that counted in the flat-racing field, he said. It was what was inherited that mattered and he ended with the ponderous aphorism that you couldn't make a silk purse out of a sow's ear, no matter how hard you tried. All of which was uncomfortably the sort of thing that had worried Leslie considerably.

"Could you lend me an evening paper?" he asked by way of changing the subject. And when Sawley returned with the paper, he asked if there was a fire in any of the public rooms.

"Oh yes, sir, there's always a fire in the lounge but not in the TV room or the little smoke-room that used to be, which they now call the bridge room. The manageress was saying she'd have the TV moved into the lounge since nobody ever sits there of an evening these days."

But there was somebody in the lounge. Miss Brown was sitting in a large over-stuffed arm-chair, reading. She took no notice at all when Leslie came in.

He sat down and opened the evening paper. He was not looking to see if there was anything about a dead woman found in a flat in Ealing because he knew there would not be. Nobody would be likely to find Lil yet. In the ordinary way, she was not home till half past six or seven, when she would at once start preparing a meal, occasionally using items of food which she brought from work. Sometimes her friends would come in for an evening meal, and more often she would go out for a meal with them, but this particular evening Leslie could think of nothing which had been planned. After supper he would watch the TV but Lil was always busy with something; making clothes for herself, doing some special cleaning, running round to a flat a few doors along where she had a friend, and she was fond of going to the cinema.

But this evening, for certain, somebody would be sent to Ealing from the bank, and, getting no reply might make inquiries from the neighbours as to when Mr. Williams usually arrived home. He tried to visualise the scene; who would be sent, which of the neighbours would he question; would he be told that both Mr. and Mrs. Williams were sure to be home shortly and hang around for hours waiting? How long would it be before somebody got panicky and suggested having the flat door opened by the maintenance man with the skeleton key? Would it be to-night? Or to-morrow morning? Or when?

Leslie stirred unhappily behind the newspaper of which he was not reading a word. Had he not been in a bit too much of a hurry this morning? Maybe if he had called a doctor and, in the meantime, tried artificial respiration, something might have been done. As it was, he had flatly accepted the situation and, without a coherent thought, had bolted. He crossed and uncrossed his legs continually and sighed noisily a number of times.

There was a small sound of a door closing and, putting down the paper, he realised that the mouse-like Miss Brown had left the room. The fire was still alight, though now low, and there was no coal box from which he could replenish it. Kneeling in front of the fireplace he crushed a handful of the evening paper, and another, and pressed them on to the hot ash. When they flared up, he brought out his cheque book and, crumpling a few pages at a time, he fed the fire with them. His cheque book was now entirely useless anyway. He and Lil had a joint account. It may be that that joint account was the root of all the trouble. Never, he told himself, *never* should married people have a joint account; it was absolutely fatal to harmony. Double beds, perhaps, never a double bank-balance. In his particular case, Lil's earnings had appeared in large dollops irregularly, completely swamping his own modest salary. And then Lil liked spending. For the last few years they had had holidays abroad which had cost sums of money far in excess of what he and his mother had lived upon for a whole year. Often they had been in the red for a short time and Lil would treat it carelessly, saying that as long as they had their health there was nothing to worry about.

If Lil wanted anything she bought it, a leopard-skin jacket, the TV, the close-fitted carpet throughout the flat, the super luggage, a crocodile handbag. And the only thing he had bought, and only after great heart-searching, had been those suède shoes from the shop in Jermyn Street.

Recently there had been talk of their buying a car on hire purchase. Lil had said that she was going to start driving lessons in the evenings as soon as the clocks were put on and that they would all (that is themselves and another couple with whom they had holidays), go abroad this year in their own car, and tour Europe. This meant that Leslie, too, would have had to have driving lessons and, when the time came, he would probably not have passed his test though Lil would have sailed through hers with something to spare.

The cheque book stubs were not burning well; he started on the passport, which was not very inflammable either. However, he did succeed, with the help of the rest of the newspaper, in inducing a fairly good blaze. He added, with great reluctance, his air ticket. He stood up and dusted the knees of his suit. The door opened as he was on his way towards it. Miss Brown came in. " Oh! " she jumped slightly. " I've left my glasses-case behind," she murmured, brushing past him. At the door he looked back and saw her thrusting her hands down between the seat cushion and the arms of the chair she had been sitting in.

" Any special time you want waking, sir? " Sawley asked from his little cubby hole in the hall.

" Seven-thirty, please, and breakfast at eight-fifteen," Leslie said firmly on his way upstairs.

" That's all right, sir. We have another gentleman, a world's worker, too. G'night, sir."

Leslie went on up.

CHAPTER III

THAT FIRST MORNING he hurried purposefully out at nine-thirty with a brisk nod to Sawley, who was now doing duty of both waiter and hall porter. It was only when he had got round the corner and out of sight of the Lugano Hotel that he slowed down. The pavements were reverberating with the tick-tock of the heels of typists as they tripped out from under the gloomy porticos down the steps and hurried towards the bus stops and tube station. All he now had to do was to hurry to Oxford Street to get a passport photograph taken. This done, a form for application for a passport had to be obtained and then the day stretched ahead in which he had nothing whatever to do but fill in time. In the next three days he went to seven films, the British Museum, the South Kensington Museums, Madame Tussaud's and Harrods.

On the Saturday he went to Brighton for the day and enjoyed it, but Sunday was difficult to expend. He went on a river trip and believed that he was enjoying himself but an eerie lethargy was overcoming him. He now had his passport photographs and the form filled in but he had not yet had it signed by two sponsors. Who was there who had known Leslie W. Dunright, and all the fictitious particulars about him, for longer than five days?

The passport problem, when squarely faced, caused a violent irritation in his mind. To go abroad now he must have a passport and he had no idea how he was to set about getting a new passport. His powers of invention were limited and his innate conventionality prevented him from thinking up some cunning scheme for obtaining one.

On Monday morning he went to the Labour Exchange. It was an experience which had upon him the effect that tempering has upon steel. He emerged from it with a hardness that was quite new; it had a far more profound influence upon him than the finding of his wife's body. At the Labour Exchange the smell, the dejected air of the men who waited with him, the indifference of the clerk who attended to him, the startling proportion of coloured men to white, and the quality of such white men as were looking for work, had the effect, as he was to say later, of " frightening him out of his wits." The only job offered him was that of sandwich-boardsman for a palmist in Oxford Street.

He came away minus two inches in height and a lot of self-respect; his suit seemed too large, his shoes shabby, everything about him diminished in quality.

A spectacularly large American car was standing parked by the pavement opposite the Labour Exchange. It was dirty and neglected-looking but Leslie paused to look at it with mild interest because it had two huge fins protruding from the back in a way which suggested that, if encouraged, it would take off into the air.

A head emerged from the window and a sharp whistle summoned him. " Looking for a job? " A man about ten years younger than himself, good-looking and flashily dressed, was eagerly addressing him. Leslie was too depressed to do anything other than stare at him dully. " I mean you. Here, get in."

" What sort of job? "

" Driving——"

Leslie shook his head. " I can't drive! "

" Strewth! " The driver of the car stared at him, gnawing his finger nails thoughtfully. " You can't drive, that's torn it," he looked restlessly from side to side. " You can't drive, eh? What can you do? "

Stung, Leslie snapped back that he could do anything within reason, for money and, he added, turning away, " within the law." He did not step into the car when invited and now he began to walk briskly along the street. He had not gone more than fifty yards, however, when the car drew up silkily alongside him and, once more, the driver put his head out and said in the richest cockney: " I got er proposition, cock." He opened the door and held it open invitingly.

Leslie hesitated; if anyone looked a spiv and thoroughly dishonest, it was the driver of the Chevrolet. To enter into any sort of dealing with him would be to desert the shores of law and order for ever, it would seem. But the spiv assured him that he was not to get him wrong. He was not asking him to do anything that was not strictly honest. No thanks, he, the spiv, had had quite enough of high jinks on the wrong side of the law in the years after the wor-er. He was now an honest-to-goodness trader; he and the police were just like that; with his clasped hands he demonstrated how close he and the police force were. Right now he was in a spot and if Leslie would kindly step in he, Charlie Cross, would tell him what it was he wanted him to do.

The back seat of the car was piled up with cardboard boxes. Mr. Cross now brought out an expensive-looking case and offered Leslie a cigarette, which he took. " Feeling more relaxed? " he asked kindly. As a matter of fact, he was, his expression showed it.

" Well, now I'll tell you what I want."

Honest Charlie Cross, there was no other appellation that fitted. He was a salesman " pure and simple." Though Leslie had no way of assuring himself upon these two conditions, he had to accept that he was also a salesman born, bred and buttered, that his father had been a salesman and his father before him. Selling was in his blood. It didn't matter what he sold, and in his time (he spoke like a man with decades of experience behind him), he had sold a great variety of things.

" And you're now going to sell me ... a pup," Leslie interjected sourly.

Charlie Cross gave a sharp bark of laughter. " Quite a sense of yumer! " he observed.

Right now he was selling shoes, a really nice line in elegant, classy, foreign footwear. And having little in the way of overheads, he was able to sacrifice these really first-class shoes at a give-away price. Now, he and his partner carried on the business turn and turn about. One week his partner would sell and Charlie would collect, next week " arsi-versi," if he understood. " And now," Charlie slumped back into the luxurious driving seat, " and now Perce has been and gorn and got himself a cor ... a cron ... a bloomin' 'art attack."

"A thrombosis? Cron-ery?"

"That's right! At his age! Not yet forty! A bloomin' great pain here struck him flat as he stepped out of bed yesday morning. His wife pretty near had kittens and now he's in hospital, having injections as make his blood run fluid, instead of clottin', see?"

Leslie didn't quite see, but never mind.

"The wife's a good kid," Charlie sucked his teeth appreciatively, "she's a good, fine kid. She's doing business in the West Country in the markets, so she's got to get around. She and a girl-friend. Well, that means there's only me left to hold this end of the business and I've got a big consignment waiting for me to collect in the East End and in the meantime I've got this lot to sell this very day, Monday."

"You thought if I could collect the goods for you, it would leave you free to sell them?"

"That's right." Charlie looked at Leslie in admiration at his powers of understanding. "That is exactly it."

"And I can't drive."

"But you might sell for me."

"Ladies' or gent's?" Leslie asked.

"At the moment it's gent's. The very best, Sunday-go-to-meetin' gent's suède footwear, Italian style."

"I don't mind having a stab at it, but you'd be disappointed; I'm no salesman."

"Have you ever tried?"

"No. Not exactly."

"Then how do you know?"

"I could *try*," he said doubtfully. "Where would it be?"

He mentioned a famous market in North-East London.

"Have you a stand there?"

Charlie looked irritable. "Stand? No, I've no permanent pitch. I drive the car up and sell off the ground; if it's wet I pull out a bit of an awning. You fussed?" From an inside pocket he drew an official form. "Pedlar's certificate," he pointed at the date; "Right up to date and tickety boo."

His manner was so phoney, yet so familiar as the brash

salesman that Leslie was bewildered. He was also excited and stimulated, on the verge of adventure. He glanced at the certificate, looking worried.

"You leave that side of it to me," Charlie winked. " I told you I'd no overheads; there's ways and means and you've got to know the ropes before you can get your foot into a market like that. I know the ropes okay. I'd take you there and leave you with the goods, and all you've got to do is to sell them."

He offered yet another cigarette which, this time, Leslie refused. "Look," Charlie decided, "let me show you——"

Stretching a long way back over the driving seat, he raised the lid of one of the boxes and brought out a pair of imitation suède shoes in mustard colour with pointed toes. They were tied together with a piece of string from the back of each heel. "You've got to get them all separated first, see, and then you're off. Look," he put on a confidential voice, "you'll never get a better, finer, more classy *and*, furthermore, a more hard-wearing shoe than this. An honest-to-goodness, first-class, genuine shoe! Look at the lining, no more sweaty feet, that's a thing of the past. Look at the eyes! Genuine plastic, no more metal eye-holes, that's another thing of the past. And as for comfort, there's nothing to touch them! Made on a special Continental last, they're designed for relaxation, put these shoes on and you forget your feet. Look at the trade mark, Ariel, messenger of the gods, fleet of foot, that's why the winged heels. You don't know you're going in this lot, believe me. And look at this——" he flexed the shoes double until toe and heel met. "Flexibility, that's what gives you the youthful, winged-heel feel. And look at this——" Turning the lining of the sole back slightly, he demonstrated a thin inter-lining of spongy material, "that's what gives you the spring. And feel the weight . . . lightness with strength . . . you're airborne in these new, *new* items of footwear. In three colours, mustard, which you see here; chocolate, a rich red-brown and . . . " he whisked out yet another pair, "nigger brown . . . and no offence to our coloured friends. By nigger I mean a rich, dark, earthy brown, and it's a term used in the trade meaning a genuine brown. But best of all, my friend, best of all! is the startling, the upset, the give-away price of, hold your breath, thirty-nine shillings and eeee . . . levenpence, only! "

Suède shoes, as it happened, were items of clothing about which Leslie felt he knew something. He took the shoe and studied it carefully. It seemed a different article altogether from the shoes he had bought for fourteen pounds in Jermyn Street, W.1, now carefully wrapped up in his case at the Lugano Hotel.

" I'll try anything once," Leslie returned at last. " And Dunright's the name. Leslie Dunright. Monday can't be a good day for selling things in a market, though? Saturday's the day, isn't it? All the men will be at work to-day."

" Pardon me, but what did you say the name was? "

" Leslie W. Dunright."

" Leslie W. Dunright, eh? What's the W. for? "

" William."

" Leslie William, eh? "

" That's right."

Charlie Cross pondered for a moment, then he returned to the question Leslie had asked.

" I'll grant you Friday and Saturday are the best days, and Sunday in Petticoat Lane. But there's always buyers around, chaps on shifts, blokes on night-work, characters loafing around with money in their pockets. It's worth it to-day, believe me, and the sooner we start the better. I'll hope to have seen the end of this lot by the time I come back."

" All these! " Leslie exclaimed. " Impossible! "

Charlie looked sly and rubbed his thumb and fore-fingers together in the classical, international sign for money, " You wantee? " he asked.

Leslie nodded emphatically. " I certainly do."

" I thought so. Well, let's cut the cackle and get going."

The market was surprisingly open; with a frolic wind blowing across the old cobbles, there was a strong reminder of the country, the site being the old cattle market of the one-time country village some five miles from London town. It was not going to rain, Charlie stated, but he insisted that Leslie wear his, Charlie's, raincoat for warmth. " You can't sell if your teeth are chattering with cold," was his opinion.

Standing in a small dug-out of boxes of shoes, in the overlong mackintosh, Leslie, though he may have looked the part as much as anyone else, felt completely out of place and extremely foolish.

" Hi, Mrs. State," Charlie called to a neighbouring stall, " Mr. Dunright . . . Mrs. State," he introduced them formally, " Mr. Dunright's obliging me——" A short conversation about the stricken Perce took place, then Charlie said he must be on his way, he had already wasted too much time. " I'll be right back just as soon as I can clear the goods," he threatened.

Mrs. State having waddled back to her own stall, he leaned forward and whispered to Leslie confidentially, but firmly, " And no funny stuff! They all know me——" He indicated the other stallholders, all, apparently, minding their own business, " and if so be you thought to get away with anything, they'd be after you like a pack of hounds! Cheerie-bye! "

On this insulting note, Charlie left Leslie to remind himself unhappily, that the warning had not been as ill-placed as all that.

For the first hour, and more, no one took the slightest notice of him, it was as though he were either invisible or inflicted with some revolting disease; he could almost imagine that people looked in his direction to look away quickly. Mrs. State came over with a cup of orange-coloured tea swabbed over into the saucer.

" 'Ow are you doing? " she asked kindly, then clicked her tongue sympathetically when she saw that he was not doing at all.

" You want to look busy, dear," she said. " As you are you look like a man's put down his parcels for a minute's rest. You want to look like you're selling. Look busy, like you've just arrived and haven't got above a few minutes before you're off elsewhere and that you'll give 'em the opportunity of buying so long as they're quick."

Mrs. State's husband, clearly a fiercely jealous type, was

urgently beckoning her back to the china and glass stall where a brisk trade was taking place. "Once you've got someone interested," she hissed, "keep the ball rolling; catch the eyes of others; hand the shoes round for inspection and keep your nose clean."

He drank his stone-cold tea wondering how on earth he was to look busy, and then remembered the string with which the shoes were tied together. He found his pocket knife, then started opening the boxes one after another, removing the string from the heels and replacing the shoes in the boxes. Then he realised that the boxes were piled up without any regard for the colour or the size of the shoes inside and at once there seemed to be a lot to do, sorting them out. No sooner had he started, however, than he found himself being watched with interest by two women.

"Ha, here you are!" he said briskly, as though they were old acquaintances, "and just in time too, madam," he smiled. "I am now on the point of giving you ladies a real tip. Look!" Proudly he put a shoe into the hand of each woman. "What do you think of that? As new as to-morrow ... you'll never find a better, finer, more classy *and*, furthermore, a more hard-wearing shoe than this. An honest-to-goodness, first-class, genuine shoe!" His voice was good and deep and strong and he liked the sound of it as it gained strength over the wind. "Look at the lining, no more sweaty feet, that's a thing of the past!" He was surprised at the cultured tone of his own voice, he sounded like a B.B.C. announcer. "And as for comfort, there's nothing to touch them." And then he launched out on his own: "This, madame," (with a slight French accent) "is a real snip; export——"

"Rejects?" one woman suggested distastefully.

"*Not* rejects, madame, *nor* seconds, but shoes made for export on an order cancelled for political reasons. You do get them, y'know, consequently they're free of purchase tax and I can offer them to you at a price that will astonish you, madame——" his voice had attracted a few other potential customers who were stretching out their necks to make sure that they were not missing anything. "It's a price you won't believe, but I'll guarantee, I'll *guarantee*, you'll be back for another pair. But then," he said sadly, " it will be too late. You won't get shoes like this, at a price like this, in a hurry again."

" Well, what is the price? " someone asked irritably.

" Thirty-nine shillings and eee . . . levenpence, only, for these fashion shoes."

" Our Mike's crazy about these Eyetalian-type shoes," one woman said in a low voice to another. " I'll 'ave one pair, size ten in mustard," she decided.

That was the start. He sold six pairs straight away. He felt, and was, clumsy about the boxes, the sizes, the colours and, finally, the lids, which started blowing about all over the place. But he took great care not to sell together shoes of different size. It was surprising that people bought without having tried them on but the fact that there was nowhere to sit whilst trying them on, discouraged them from asking if they might.

Eye-appeal, that was it. He had heard of the importance of this in modern trading and here was something that, he privately considered, had little to recommend it other than eye-appeal. They proclaimed themselves at a glance to be luxury goods. Though he did not know it, he was more than ordinarily successful because of his appearance. He looked and spoke like a gentleman; healthy and clean and reasonably well-groomed, he was not the type to sell anybody anything that was shoddy and not worth having. The salesman, as well as the shoes, had eye-appeal.

By five-thirty he had sold the astonishing number of eighty-three pairs, seven dozen, and there remained only one box, containing two shoes of odd colours which had somehow been included accidentally. He tidied up the litter that lay around his feet and walked across to his friend Mrs. State like a pack-mule, his pockets bulging with paper money.

Mrs. State smiled at him proudly. " See? New to it, aren't you? I could tell that at once. But you're a born salesman. They can see you're not havin' them on, straight-up, they can. That's what I always say; the public knows; you can't fool them. Your salesman is the chap that knows he's giving value for money and no kiddin'. What you goin' to do with that last pair of shoes, dear?"

"Sell one each to two one-legged men," Leslie returned snappily and in the laugh that followed, his friendship with Mrs. State was sealed.

If he was pleased, Charlie Cross showed no sign of it. He turned up shortly before six with the back of the car piled to the roof with new stock. "Jeez, it's a lot more tiring driving through London all day than it is selling, believe me," he said. "I've had near on four hours of it but I'll drive you back to the Metrop. I live S.W. way. Where would you like to be dropped?"

At the Lugano Hotel, which was almost on his way. Why not? But when they got into the car and Leslie handed over the money he had taken, Charlie counted through it briskly yet carefully.

"Right, to the last penny," he stated.

"I should hope so," Leslie remarked and immediately regretted having done so when Charlie gave him a sharp look before counting out twenty pound notes and two half crowns. "There you are! It's a lot more than it pays me to give you but since you obliged, out of the blue, like that——"

A long slow drive back to Gloucester Road through the City and the rush-hour traffic; it was a few minutes before seven when they drew up at the Lugano. Leslie could see Sawley, now in his white waiter's jacket, standing with his hands behind his back, idly looking out through the glass panels of the front door.

Charlie looked appraisingly at the frontage of the hotel. "So this is where you live, is it?"

"Where I'm staying for a week or two."

Charlie inhaled deeply from his newly-lighted cigarette. "Well, Les old cock, there's no questions asked but I don't mind saying I don't trust you any farther than I could kick you."

It was said so pleasantly that Leslie had difficulty, for a moment, in grasping what he had said. He was one who was slow to anger and, deeply imbued with guilt, he said nothing in return. He used the ample ash-tray for the stub of his own cigarette and attempted to open the door.

"Allow me," Charlie leaned across and manipulated the door catch. "But not to worry," he went on, "you look as honest as the Bank of England. You *look* honest . . . I *am* honest. With your looks and my brains we ought to get some place, together."

Leslie stepped out; the driving wheel being on the port side, he had to make the long walk round the monstrous car to reach the pavement. This he did with a studied dignity.

"So long, Les, old cock," Charlie shouted from the lowered window. "And ta a lot!"

With the dignity of the Prime Minister acknowledging the crowds from the steps of ten Downing Street, Leslie raised a hand in farewell before disappearing from view through the door that Sawley was holding wide open for him.

CHAPTER IV

MISS LYNEAUX was in the hall. In a tight-fitting black suit and a tiny pink hat made entirely of flowers, she was lounging gracefully over the reception counter in Sawley's little cubby hole, looking through her mail.

What Leslie wanted more than anything else in the world, was a drink. As the Lugano had no licence it was clear that he would have to go out again to the nearest pub but he would give Charlie Cross time to drive off and away; to re-emerge too quickly would be to cause an anti-climax. He had thrust the money he had earned into his jacket pocket and now he brought out his pocket book from his hip pocket and slid the notes carefully and tidily away.

"Had a busy day, Mr. Dunright?" Miss Lyneaux, looking at him over her shoulder with her strange green eyes, reminded him strongly of a tortoiseshell cat, not the sort with a full face and contented eyes but a tortoiseshell cat with a lean small face and worried eyes, such as he had often seen on the Continent.

"Very busy," he said, "I'm tired! Pity they haven't a bar here."

"Oh, but there's The Mermaid Bar at the Double Gloucester. Just re-opened after its face-lift. It's quite fun provided you can stand the fishy atmosphere. Fish everywhere, in the ground glass screens, and all over the walls, and there's even a large tank of them, opening and shutting their mouths at you," she laughed, "showing you how to drink."

"Where is it?"

"One minute away! Come along, I'll take you." Suddenly she had a laughing merry face and her hand was held out to him. He was at once infected by this onset of the party spirit. Hand-in-hand they ran down the steps and on to the pavement. He immediately detached himself and was glad he had done so. Miss Hermione Brown was standing staring down into the area. She looked up at once and said: "Oh, dear. That little black cat! I wonder if something has happened to her. I haven't seen her for over a week. She's always here to greet me when I get home at six. You haven't seen her, either of you, have you?"

"There's lots and lots of black cats, Miss Brown," Miss Lyneaux cried cheerfully.

"But this was rather a special one," Miss Brown returned sadly, "she has one brown eye and one green and she's always been unlucky. One of her ears is in ribbons and the end of her tail has gone!"

"She'll be ' scrambling for fish heads in an alley '," Miss Lyneaux called, apparently meaninglessly, over her shoulder and laughed excitedly. "Crazy old spinsters and their cats," she said in a low voice as they walked on. "It's the only thing she ever thinks about. She's built that blasted cat a kind of bower down there in the basement area beside the dustbins, with a cardboard roof and an old jumper to sit on, and in the winter she puts out a hot water bottle under the jumper! Aren't some people crazy!"

Remembering with a slight start that he *had* seen Miss

Brown's cat for a split second Leslie said nothing because they now arrived at The Mermaid Bar.

His wife Lil and her friends had always demanded impeccable manners from their husbands and their friends' husbands; Leslie was an old hand at finding somewhere for the ladies to sit, pulling out chairs, helping them off with their coats, providing them with cigarettes and asking them what they would have to drink. Miss Lyneaux flowered under his ministrations. She wanted a White Lady.

But standing at the bar whilst the girl mixed two White Ladies, Leslie fell a victim to an attack of thought to which, in the last few days, he had been uncomfortably prone. *There are more ways of murdering than by giving the poison*, he thought, *you're just as much a murderer if you cause someone to give themselves the poison*, and the thought was so enervating that he quickly drank one White Lady and ordered another.

"Here's happiness!" Miss Lyneaux twinkled at him over her glass. "You can call me Elizabeth, if you like."

"And you can call me Leslie," he returned gallantly.

When they say "all women," men usually mean all the women they have met since they were eighteen or so; Leslie was by no means overstating the case when he told himself that *all women* within the first few minutes of acquaintance by subtle means or by asking outright, attempted to find out if he was married or not. All women were so darned personal, he told himself. He was proud, in a self-congratulatory way, to have at least come across a woman who was not like that. Not that he was unprepared for the question, he had been working out the answer to that one for many months. But it was flattering not to be asked and somehow it lifted this acquaintanceship out of the ordinary run and put it on a plane somewhat higher than any he had so far experienced.

She was a woman who was used to the company of men; forthright and intelligent. They discussed politics for the first couple of drinks. She had been a W.R.E.N. officer in the war and had been closely connected with the signing of the Atlantic Treaty; she could not, of course, say how closely but he understood that it was pretty close. As Leslie had been found unfit for National Service owing to varicose veins, to his very great chagrin, he was desperately grateful to her for not looking keenly at him with her green eyes and asking what he had done in the war. She seemed to take it for granted that he, too, had been intimately associated with the running of it, however, and he played up to this in great goodhumour.

The Mermaid barman certainly fixed an excellent White Lady. Leslie was in a happy position of being able absolutely to forbid her from standing a round; this was his party.

With the third round, Miss Lyneaux laughingly confessed that she was lazy; the war had taken everything out of her; she had given her youth to her country and there was not much of her left, these days.

Taking his cue, Leslie said all the right things.

Actually, she was looking for a flat. Until her old father had died, some years ago now, she had lived with him in a variety of hotels. When he died there was no longer any need for her to go on living at the Lugano, but could she find the right flat? She had spent days and days flat-hunting, walked miles and miles, without success. Living at the Lugano had its compensations; it left her free to go away, to go in and out as and when she wanted. She had her own small car and could go places anytime without the worries she would have in leaving a flat.

" And wouldn't you be lonely, living in a flat all by yourself? "

" Yes," she admitted, " there is that! "

She went on to discuss the other residents at the Lugano. They were not exactly lively but they were not too bad; there was no one in the hotel who was a particular nuisance. The single old man with paralysis agitans had been a friend of her father and was now too taken up with his weakness to attend much to anything else. The bored young man who sat alone usually reading the *New Statesman* was a physicist; he had been transferred to London from the provinces and was entirely occupied in his spare time in looking for somewhere for his wife and family to live; he went home every week-end, anyway.

" And Miss Brown? "

Miss Lyneaux gave a tinkling laugh. " She's our old eccentric! "

" Not old, surely! "

" Getting on, my dear. She's a world's worker . . . I'm afraid she hasn't much time for me. She thinks I'm flippant and tiresome, dear old Hermione Brown. She's one of the assistants at the New Century Book Club, a famous lending library in Grosvenor Square; she's worked on Desk W to Z for years and years. I ask you! " Miss Lyneaux's laugh tinkled out again. " I wonder how she gets on with all the X's! " She was convulsed with laughter but Leslie did not quite see the joke.

" She's got pretty hair," he murmured uncomfortably.

Miss Lyneaux pulled herself together. She dabbed the tears of laughter from the corners of her eyes, patted her hair and brushed away any specks of fluff from the lapels of her beautifully tailored suit.

" Oh yes, very pretty hair," she agreed soberly. " Beautifully thick, shiny hair; I shouldn't wonder if it's down to that tiny waist of hers. My mother had hair like that. My father often used to tell me that, when they were married, Mother could sit on her hair." Miss Lyneaux again shook with laughter, so much so that Leslie looked nervously at the clock, over the big fish tank, and wondered if perhaps they had stayed too long.

" Can you imagine," she choked with laughter and started again: " Can you imagine why, in those days, they thought it an advantage to be able to sit on their hair? "

" Come on," Leslie suggested, uncomfortable in case they were making themselves conspicuous. " Let's go out and have dinner up west. We're far too late for dinner at the Lugano; we'll go to that new Chinese Restaurant, shall we? "

Next morning he was up, breakfasted and ready in good time for the telephone call he positively knew he would be having from Charlie Cross. He sat in the hall and read through *The Times* in a position that was well within earshot of the telephone.

When Sawley's duties as waiter were over, he changed into his blue jacket and came back to his cubby-hole in the hall. First Miss Brown and then the physicist went off to work. The old people, unable to return upstairs until after their rooms had been cleaned, wandered to and fro restlessly with polite " good mornings " and comments on the weather. The old men shuffled out on to the top step and surveyed the weather for themselves, casting their eyes up to the great black-bellied clouds overhead, shaking their heads and saying that perhaps they wouldn't risk it yet awhile. Two of them told Leslie that April showers bring May flowers and one of them, with a twinkle in his eye, said: " Oh, to be in England now that April's there," and Leslie, for the first time for twenty-four hours, reminded himself that he would much rather be in Paris and, in fact and with luck, would be in Paris before long.

He borrowed Sawley's *Daily Mirror* and looked through it. *Suppose she hadn't been dead? Suppose she had been in a coma as the result of what she had taken? If he had got her into hospital they might have saved her, with stomach pumps and stimulants. As it was, how long could it have been before she was found? Was it possible that she could still be lying there, after a week?*

" Taking a day off, sir? " Sawley asked.

" Oh dear me no! I'm waiting for a telephone call . . . or someone may call in person."

" Pity. Races at Brighton to-day. Make a nice day's outing," Sawley mused, his kindly eyes behind the spectacles which he wore for reading remaining fixed upon the fixture list. He hummed lightly.

" Got any tips? " Leslie asked with the jocularity of the bank clerk when on the subject of betting.

" Only a red-hot job in the three-thirty. But horse racing doesn't interest you, sir."

" Oh, I dunno! "

" This field is a lot of cat's meat, as it happens, and Moonshine'd win with a bulldozer tied on behind, honest and straight-up he would."

" I'd never back a horse with a name like that! "

This was the signal for Sawley to break out into some

exceedingly knowledgeable information about Moonshine's ancestry. Out of the wonderful mare Moonstruck and granddaughter of the world-famous Ladymoon, the one sold to the Maharaja of Purjar for fifty thousand. Well, this here Moonshine was off to a bad start at the beginning of the flat season, been a very great disappointment to her owner who had got rid of her for a paltry sum to a trainer who had kept her very much as his second string. She hadn't run yet this season but she'd shown her paces on the training ground.

" How can you know? "

Naturally enough, Sawley did not explain how he knew. He started a long dissertation about odds which Leslie cut short. " Don't know a thing about it; don't know one end of a horse from the other. But you can put this on for me, if you like." He took a pound note out of his wallet and handed it over.

" Now, sir," Sawley said reprovingly, " I don't want to start nothink."

" That's all right." Leslie gave a wave of his hand to show how little it meant to him.

Among his many assets Charlie Cross was a natural psychologist. It would have been a mistake to telephone to, or call for Leslie the day after he had done so well in the market. That way blokes got too cocky, he told Leslie later, too sure that they were indispensable. He gave no sign at all of his continued existence until Friday.

In the meantime the friendship with Miss Lyneaux, as Leslie phrased it to himself, ripened. He found her stimulating, her conversation fascinated him. Nobody of his acquaintance had ever talked like she talked, uninhibited and amusing; he never knew what she was going to say next. For instance, picking up a newspaper which was lying in The Mermaid Bar, she pointed out a photograph of a famous broadcaster, a man with a tremendous growth of hair on his upper lip. In this instance he was advertising a make of cigarette; with a straight look, he was handing a packet of cigarettes to the camera.

" Isn't he sweet! God! I adore men with moustaches like

that! But, my dear!" she laughed, "how does he smoke without setting his face on fire? I bet he's a non-smoker; I mean, he couldn't, could he?"

Leslie was appalled to hear her saying: "I should guess being kissed by him would be like being kissed by one of those fluffy bedside rugs!"

Bedside rug! And the basin of vomit! She must have got up out of bed to get the basin and got back again. Wasn't that oddly inexplicable? Why was it that only now he should begin to see the whole experience of finding his wife dead, in a more detailed light?

"Oh, you old sober-sides! Why not laugh? It was meant to be funny!"

When opportunity offered, he went to a barber's in one of the little streets behind Bond Street and had a haircut. Afterwards he had a discussion with the barber. In the man's opinion, he could never grow a luxurious moustache like that of a famous back-bencher in the House of Commons. "It'd turn out wispy, if you don't mind my saying so, sir."

"Oh dear me no! I asked for your opinion."

"You're not a hairy gentleman, if you know what I mean. Probably quite bald when you was a kiddy, or I should say, a baby-in-arms. And, if you don't mind my saying so, sir, it won't be long before you're bald again."

Leslie nodded, depressed. "I see exactly what you mean. I quite understand."

"In the army, sir?" the barber asked briskly.

Leslie, flattered, denied that he was in the regular army.

"Pity. A nice little moustache," the barber demonstrated with two fingers below his own nostrils, ". . . there . . . would be just the job. Distinguished. It would suit you, believe me."

So it would, so it would!

By Thursday evening, Leslie had quite lost hope in Charlie Cross. He was wondering how soon he could get his new passport form properly filled-in when, on Friday morning, he was called from breakfast to the telephone; Charlie would come for him in an hour's time, okey dokey?

And then, as the car stood outside with Charlie pip-pipping the horn, Sawley stopped him. "One minute, sir, begging your pardon." He rummaged about in his desk drawer and finally brought out an envelope, unsealed and unaddressed. "Yours, sir."

"What's this?" Leslie had that morning tipped Sawley liberally. The five-pound note in the envelope made it seem as though Sawley were tipping him.

"Your winnings, sir. Sorry, I haven't had time to go round and collect before now."

For a moment, Leslie hadn't the slightest idea what he was talking about.

"Moonshine, sir. The horse."

"Good heavens! I'd forgotten all about it. Thanks very much, Sawley."

"Anytime, sir, anytime."

In no single week of his life had Leslie received so much money ... and for so little. He ran down the steps and got into the fantastic car, fingering the place where his small moustache had started to grow, to hide the smile on his lips.

"I suppose you haven't seen my little black cat anywhere about, have you, Mr. Dunright?"

"No, Miss Brown. I'm afraid I haven't." How could he tell her that her little black cat had certainly died of a ruptured spleen behind some alien dustbin?

"You see, we aren't allowed to keep any pets here in the hotel, and one can understand that. But I made a little home for her down in the area. She always used to come back. She learned to climb up to my balcony; she was there every morning when I took out her milk. And she was always waiting for me when I came home from work." She lowered her voice. "Of course, there have been times when she has come up through the hotel to my room to look for me, but she was always careful to keep out of Sawley's way. She moved quickly and kept in the shadows; she was like a quick little shadow herself."

"Perhaps you'll find another little cat to befriend," Leslie suggested kindly.

"Oh, yes, there are lots and lots of cats about who need

help and friendship but that won't explain what has happened to this little friend, will it? I know she would never have not come back, just like that. I'm sure there's something wrong."

And so, in a lull in Friday's bustle of selling, when Mrs. State came waddling over with the orange-coloured tea slopped over into the saucer, Leslie asked her if she knew of anybody with any kittens of which they wanted to be rid.

" Bless you, there's thousands to be had for the asking."

" I know. Now I'm doing the asking."

" When do you want it ? "

" Soon as maybe. And a black one if poss."

" I'll see what I can do," Mrs. State said.

On Sunday morning, when Leslie was standing on the doorstep and wondering whether Miss Lyneaux would be available for a walk across the park in the weak spring sunshine, the now familiar car drew up and a dark and angry face looked out at him.

" Well, thank God you're there." Charlie thrust an arm out of the window. His hand contained a scratching and struggling kitten.

" Are you crazy! " he asked, not caring to hear the answer. " Mrs. State landed me with this lot yesday afternoon when trade was at its best. For God's sake take it off of me, it's torn the lining of my coat pocket to ribbons, very near fallen through and got trod on."

But Charlie had much too much respect for Leslie as a salesman to tear him to ribbons. On the whole, he treated the episode with a tolerant amusement but made it quite clear that it must not occur again. If it should happen again, next time he'd wring its bloody neck. He really hadn't got time for carry-ons of that kind on the part of his employees, he'd got too much on his mind, see?

Leslie apologised.

Charlie rubbed his nose on the back of his thick finger and pushed his hat to the back of his head. " I'm off to see Perce, at St. Bartholomew's Hospital, see how he's gettin' on. Look, Les, if Perce is out for the count, and I'm pretty sure he is, could you do me teapots ? "

"Teapots?"

"A new line in genuine teapots."

"I said I'd try anything once. What day?"

"Thursday. I'll run you there, same pitch, same time. Right?"

The car shot away from the pavement like a sky-blue rocket and Leslie was left with a burning feeling between his shoulders where he knew Sawley, from the doorway, was looking and it was biting in. An even more painful burning feeling came from his hand where the kitten was beginning to claw a pattern on it. Turning abruptly, he thrust the kitten into the pocket of his best suit and walked rapidly along the road.

He swore. This was where a casual kindly thought led you. If Elizabeth should come out now and see him, how she would jeer! How could he have made such a sentimental ass of himself? He was strongly tempted to strangle the beastly thing and thrust it through the grating of the gutter into the drain. Two things only stopped him: the first was that he would hate to hurt the horrid kitten and secondly, the knowledge that he needed to build up a background round Leslie Dunright because Mr. Dunright needed friends as much or even more than most people need friends. And anyway, he liked Miss Brown. If only she would come out now.

But he had not seen her all morning and in desperation he went into The Mermaid and sought the help of the barmaid. "It's a surprise for someone; if you could keep it for me for an hour or so, I promise it won't be long——"

So the barmaid, grumbling but nevertheless helpful, put it into a basket, tied a cloth over the top and left it mewing loudly, in the staff lavatory.

He was first in to lunch at the Lugano, leaving a note in Miss Brown's place: "Meet me at The Mermaid at two, please. L. Dunright." If Sawley saw the manœuvre of putting the note unobtrusively on Miss Brown's plate, he gave no sign but he did murmur: "Miss Lino's out to lunch with friends," which knowledge made things considerably easier.

Staring ahead, Leslie could, from the side of his eye, see Miss Brown open the note and read it. After a few moments, when he looked directly at her, he could see that she had flushed.

But when she saw the kitten she almost wept.

" I'm so sorry it isn't a black one," Leslie apologised, " but it has rather sweet blue eyes, hasn't it? "

" Oh, Mr. Dunright, you're a cat-lover too! "

He denied it instantly and indignantly.

" But how on earth are you going to cope with it? It will never stay in the little hide-out you've made! "

" You can leave that to me. Sawley is off this afternoon but right now he's clearing up the dining-room; it always takes him longer after Sunday lunch. Please go back now and keep *cave*, Mr. Dunright, and I'll creep upstairs with it, behind his back."

" Keep what? "

" Perhaps you could talk to Sawley, that would be even better. So then I can creep in unnoticed."

Miss Brown tucked the kitten firmly under her arm inside the jacket of her suit. It was already a good deal quieter, it looked contented and would at any moment start to purr. " Thank you, Mr. Dunright. You are a most, most kind man! "

Kind? If he were kind he would have done something for his poor Lil. Other people were kind, not he. The kind people in the flats around would have noticed something wrong, for sure. By now they would have got the caretaker to open the flat door. Except that they minded their own business. It couldn't possibly happen that Lil was still lying there, her face covered by the sheet?

CHAPTER V

CHARLIE CROSS was one of those people who seem to have been born with a car around them; they are rarely seen to walk and when they do so, they have the incongruity of a tortoise progressing without its shell. Charlie, walking ahead of him, struck a curious, dimly flickering light in Leslie's brain. He had seen him before for sure. Or was it that Charlie was a type, with his lean hips, his wide shoulders, his teddy-bear coat with the sash belt, and his odd way of walking with his feet turned in slightly and an exaggerated planting of the heels down first? Had he seen him before or was it simply that he had seen so many like him?

The teapots were made of some nameless metal that looked very like silver and cost twenty-one and ninepence. Learning from Charlie that any article you required to " sell a lot of, and quickly," must be new, that is, must be in some way different from what had gone before; Leslie quickly registered what was new about them. The metal was new, quite new to him anyway. The lid slid off backwards instead of having to be taken off, or lifted back on a hinge. The handles were in plastic of different colours and were fixed on to the body of the teapot in a very new way. The spout was merely an extension of a hole in the side of the teapot which seemed to mean that no flaw could occur between the teapot and the spout; very new indeed. But the newest idea of all was a small container of thin wire mesh, which could be withdrawn from the teapot by a tiny chain; this was for the tea-leaves and was a labour-saving device in that it could be emptied without the labour of turning upside-down the whole teapot; it was also an economy scheme because nobody could use more tea-leaves than were actually required, though they could use less.

" New, that's what sells; you can sell anything so long as it's new," Charlie told him. " New houses, new designs, new developments, new devices, new methods, new any bloody thing ... keep that word in your head ... NEW ... and you're on the up-and-up. It was the key word to the fifties and, please the Lord, it will be the key word to the sixties and is as important to the salesman as the ignition key of his car. If our old Perce dies which, please the Lord, he won't, the last word he'll utter will be ' NEW '."

He laughed to show how familiar the thought of death was to him, then sobered up quickly and became philosophical. His occasional bursts of philosophy sat ill upon him but were uttered in the same pious way as when he had declared his relations with the police. He could not afford to be on the wrong side of God any more than he could afford to be on the wrong side of the police and, apparently, the illness of his friend and partner Perce had brought this home even more closely to him.

"Between you and me, Les," Charlie went on, " there's nothink new under the sun, and when you shout your head off about NEW, you're creating a ... an ... illusion ... and illusion is the egg-head word for kidding yourself; I've looked it up in a bloomin' dictionary, so I know. And that's what we all live on these days. We've had it, all of us, and now we live on kiddin' ourselves. Right."

At least ten years younger than Leslie, Charlie Cross talked like an elderly disillusioned man-of-the-world, and delivered it all in a semi-refined cockney. He was himself an illusion because, though he looked a very up-to-the-minute, prosperous, good-looking business-man (just slightly off-side), he was, in fact, a genuine, sharp-witted, clever pedlar, born within the sound of Bow Bells with that ability to observe and comment upon Life that was inherent in his cockney ancestors who had stood by and watched the peasants burn down John of Gaunt's Savoy Palace.

But life was not for Leslie to comment upon; he only wanted to live it, albeit to live it *his* way, but he listened to everything that Charlie said because he had a mild wish to learn.

He watched Charlie walking back to the car with that same odd feeling of familiarity, then turned to his stock. He was standing in a butt of packing cases, the target of all eyes;

there were interested on-lookers standing in front of his position before he had taken out the first few teapots, unwrapped them, removed the scraps of straw that adhered to them and put them carefully on the cobbles in front of his feet.

He started selling at once, even before he was through with his splendid demonstration of the *newness* of the teapot. When opportunity offered he went over to Mrs. State, at the china stall, and thanked her for the kitten.

" That's all right, dear. Fond of cats, are you? "

No, Leslie was not fond of cats, but he had a friend who was.

Mrs. State understood perfectly. It had been no trouble at all; the lady next door had friends whose auntie had a cat which was always having kittens and she'd asked for somebody to take the last lot out in a sack and drown them for her. Quite a coincidence, wasn't it? Was his friend satisfied with the kitten? Sorry it couldn't be a blackie, but there it was.

Leslie asked if he could pay for it but Mrs. State waved this aside, saying certainly not, it was a pleasure, anytime.

When Charlie Cross returned at six, there was an over-spill of eighteen teapots which, together, they sold at the knock-down, give away, all-time low price of twelve-and-sixpence.

Success was having a heady effect, like strong, delicious wine but more lasting, upon the newly-made Leslie Dunright. His moustache had achieved the status of what the barber called " half-guards " though it was not, in fact, shrubby enough to curl upwards when the hot tongs were applied. He now wore his suède shoes every day, except when he was working. He bought himself a dashing half-length white nylon mackintosh and, for the present, the Paris plan was shelved and the uncompleted passport form lay disregarded in his bulging wallet along with all the money he was making.

From time to time he reviewed his situation. Nobody in the whole over-populated world knew, or could possibly know, that Mr. Leslie Dunright of the Lugano Hotel, South Kensington, was Mr. Leslie Williams of the City and Suburban Bank. As time went by he became more impressed by this fact. Though he was only a few miles from his home and from his place of work he was more lost to both than if he were a newly-arrived Englishman in Paris, New York or Rio. Though in Paris he would be anonymous, in London he was even more so because there were so many like him; he was merely that one ant amongst those millions of other ants.

A splendid feeling of confidence was growing inside him and at the same time he found himself thinking more and more about Miss Elizabeth Lyneaux; one evening that relationship came to a head. They were having one of those delightful *intime* little dinners in Soho which had become a habit and which so nearly came up to the many dinners he would have had in small Paris restaurants if, as he put it, fate had not intervened.

Up to now, Miss Lyneaux had enjoyed talking about herself a great deal more than she enjoyed talking about him, but this, as it happened, was exactly as it should be. She talked so entertainingly that she never bored him but, as time went on, the apparent lack of interest in his personal life became almost unnatural. If they were to become any more intimate, she would have to know something about him, otherwise it wouldn't be, as he put it, " quite nice." He had no outstanding powers of invention; he was unable, in fact, to rise very much above the simple truth; it was only geographically that he let himself go. He told her that he was a widower and she said that she had thought so; had he been a widower long? And he said no, and she said that that, too, she had guessed because he had, somehow, looked so stricken the first day she had seen him. It was said so kindly and sympathetically that he had gone on to tell her that he worked in a bank, and had done for the past twenty years. That he had been married to a woman who could not have children and this had so preyed upon her mind that one day she had taken an overdose of sleeping tablets. " It was her time of life," he went on, " poor soul."

Miss Lyneaux was shocked. " She died beside you in bed ? "

" No. I came home from the bank and found her."

" Oh, you poor dear! "

" There has always been a woman in my life," he heard with astonishment himself say, " My mother and I were all in all to each other, and when she died I couldn't wait to marry; I married the very next girl I met, woman, rather; Lil was older than me." (He did not say by how much.)

"Your father died when you were young?"

"I was ten. Father worked in a bank, like me, and like his father before him. But one day, coming in through the front gate, he dropped down with a pain here, and died within an hour, before our eyes, and he was only forty-three. It was at the new house we'd rented on a hill and Father had to walk up home from the station. As he'd always sat at a bank counter and never took any exercise, that was what did it."

"Where was this?"

He thought. He could not say: Muswell Hill. What other place was hilly? Bath, but there was no need to say it.

"In the West of England," he replied and she left it at that.

"My poor dear. You're the sort of man who needs a woman, I saw that at once, and not necessarily in a sexual way."

He was shocked but he protested that she wasn't quite right there. Was she laughing at him? Making fun of him? He looked at her anxiously.

"You're sweet, Leslie, perfectly sweet but you've led a very sheltered life, haven't you? I can see that."

He protested again.

"It stands out a mile, dear. You're good-looking and yet so innocent-looking."

"Oh, I say! Come off it."

"That Lil of yours didn't flatter you, did she? She never told you you are good-looking, did she?"

"She didn't think so."

"Well, I do. You're far too good-looking to let life pass you by."

"But that's just what it has been doing," he returned eagerly.

"Heroes of novels aren't always good-looking. But have you noticed, how heroines of novels always are?"

"I don't read novels, so I don't know."

"Don't read novels! What do you read?"

"Me? I've no time for reading!"

"Well, let me tell you; heroines of novels are always

beautiful and highly-sexed. And if they are highly-sexed without being beautiful, they are called 'nymphomaniacs.' That word was never used outside a psychiatrist's consulting room; now it's a household word used for anyone who likes an occasional roll in the hay . . . fairly often."

He rose splendidly to the occasion. Swallowing all his prejudices in one big gulp of brandy he responded magnificently: " Like you? "

Much later, because Sawley was fussy and liked almost to tuck up his charges in bed before turning out the lights finally, they lay in bed as close together as two halves of a walnut but even then she was discursive. " Isn't it funny," she went on, " in books, and in plays, and on the films, they have always got to be boosted up with alcohol before they can get round to making love. You know there's going to be a terrific love-scene when the man picks up the telephone receiver and orders the room-service to send up champagne. But we don't need that, do we? "

He couldn't agree. With the wine they had had for dinner and the subsequent brandy still coursing round in his blood, he couldn't agree.

" What did you say, darling? " she asked.

" I said, ' Oh, I don't know '."

He awoke some hours later; the bedside light was still on and, realising he was in bed with a strange woman, his body gave an involuntary start and he leaped from the bed with an automatically murmured apology, as instinctively as he would have disengaged on finding himself standing on a passenger's foot in a crowded tube. She was lying on her side, turned away from him, in the large single bed.

The jacket of her black suit was hanging from a coat-hanger on the edge of her wardrobe. Her skirt on a skirt-hanger. Her little pink hat and black gloves were on the dressing table; her " smalls," as he called them, neatly folded on a chair. Leslie was now wearing only his cotton vest; the rest of his clothes he saw, with mild shock, were lying about all over the room in positions of wild abandon.

Even his suède shoes had lost their dignity, standing beside the bed, pigeon-toed into the form of an inverted V.

He dressed, leaving his shirt-collar unbuttoned but, when he noticed himself in the dressing-table mirror, he found he looked so wildly dissipated that, even for the return to his own room, he put on his tie and combed his hair. His wrist watch told him it was ten to three and, though he was hardly likely to meet anyone on the short journey back, he felt better. He touched his hip pocket to make sure his wallet was safe, then went towards the bed with the idea of turning out the bedside lamp.

Her defenceless face was turned to the light. His heart gave a great jerk; she seemed to be so still, not breathing, and he leaned closer so that his face was only a foot or so from hers. Then suddenly her eyes opened. She stretched luxuriously and sat up. Her hair, which he had at first thought faded, was now standing out all round her head, making her face look even smaller and more pointed.

" What's the hurry ? " she asked, adding : " You dear little man."

" I must go," he returned formally, glancing at his wrist watch as though ending an interview.

" Come here first." He sat down on the edge of the bed, always an awkward position when the person in the bed wishes to kiss the percher. She pulled him sideways and kissed him roundly and he unhappily wished the light were out.

" Would you still say I was a nympho ? "

Alcohol had now been coursing gaily round in his blood stream for seven hours and was rapidly ceasing to do so. He wanted to get back to his room, to be alone.

" No answer. Anyway, I'm not beautiful, you must admit that. Look, my hair begins far too far back. And all these freckles——"

" Oh, shut up ! " He kissed her roughly.

" Why not stay ? " She patted the narrow stretch of bed beside her.

It was Lil who had said they must have twin beds. " Nobody has double beds these days," she had said, " it's disgusting! Old fashioned! " Perhaps that had been the beginning of the trouble.

A single bed is an island and if your marriage begins to go wrong, there you are, marooned! he thought unhappily.

"Cheer up, little man. You haven't gone to the devil. We're not really doing anything wrong or hurting anybody. We're going to have lots of fun together, you and me!"

She snuggled down under the clothes and looked up at him happily. On the way back to his room the stairs creaked loudly and outside Miss Brown's room, which was near his own, one of his ankle bones went off with a crack that sounded to him as loud as a revolver shot.

CHAPTER VI

... BUT JOY cometh with the morning.

When he got up he felt as newly-created as an ordinary fruit cake that has been iced and, as he sprang past Sawley on his way out to buy newspapers, he felt acutely self-conscious.

"Seen the results, sir?" Sawley asked when he got back.

"No, I never remember to look at the results. Why?"

"That Moonshine, sir. Came in first at Hurst Park. But she was favourite; the odds went right down. Now if you'd put somethink on that time you won, for this race, you'd have got ten to one!"

"Would I really?"

Sawley went on to explain that if the filly was running again at this meeting, she would be worth backing, even at two to one. "You'd double your money."

Leslie withdrew for a moment and extracted five pounds from his wallet. "Here, put this on for me, will you?"

There followed some discussion about Leslie's double room for which he was at present paying the full price. Sawley explained that what he had had in mind was the physicist leaving, having found a home for himself and his family. "Then you could have his room, sir. That is, if you had it in mind to stay on for a bit. I had the idea you was on your way."

"I am," Leslie returned emphatically, "I am on my

way but there's some business cropped up that I must attend to in London first. I'll keep on the room I have, for the time being. I take it that you'd have no difficulty in re-letting it if I left? "

" Oh, none at all, sir."

" At a moment's notice? "

" None at all! "

Why did I say that? Why should I leave at a moment's notice? There's nothing against Leslie Dunright, nothing whatever.

Sawley had been studying some racing news in his paper. Now he straightened up, took off his glasses and looked directly at Leslie. " Would you be thinking of leaving at a moment's notice? "

" Not necessarily; but these things do happen sometimes."

With a sudden coldness about his elated heart, Leslie withdrew to the lounge. There were a few minutes to go still to breakfast time. The shaky old gentleman, also an early riser, was sitting in an arm-chair with his newspaper open in front of him. Leslie sat down, too, and opened one of his newspapers. Presently the old gentleman began to click his tongue. " Tck tck tck! I see there has been another horrid murder."

Leslie cleared his throat.

" This time it's a girl stabbed outside a dance hall, dear me! How tired one gets of it and yet it's no good shutting one's eyes to it." He thumped the overstuffed arm of his chair feebly. " It's what I've always said . . . psychiatrists can't cure crime; there's only one thing that will cure crime and that's policemen. Double the police force; double their pay; and we'll halve crime."

" Do you think so? "

" Of course I think so . . . all those young hooligans waving knives outside dance halls in the small hours . . . have a small army of police in the vicinity and you'd soon wipe out all that! "

The matter was not thrown open to discussion; that depression which dogmatism always gave him was beginning to steal over him when the old gentleman startled him by saying:

"And what was going on last night? Did you hear anything?"

"Me?" Leslie could only shake his head vaguely.

"There was such a stampede outside my door I thought we'd got a gang of teddy-boys on board!" he complained shrilly.

Stampede. Could it possibly have sounded like a stampede?

The old man put down his paper and looked across at Leslie, shaking a forefinger like a schoolmaster: "But I have my ideas!" Leslie shrank. "Oh yes! I have my ideas!"

What sort of reply was possible to such a remark? "So have I," he said boldly.

"But she'll be found out, mark my words, she'll be found out! Believe me, you can't carry on like that and get away with it indefinitely."

"I absolutely agree," Leslie said, "I'm with you there."

The old man, with small groans and sighs, rose from the depths of his chair and approached Leslie. "It is a pity the Powers-that-Be is away; and by that I mean the manageress here. She's gone off on her honeymoon to the Antipodes," he blew out his cheeks to show how absurd such an action was, "and the place is going to pot in her absence. However——" he straightened up in a soldierly manner, as best he could, "if it goes on, I shall be forced to interfere. Reluctantly . . . but nevertheless . . . it will be my duty."

And he shuffled off.

Over porridge, kipper, toast and marmalade, a series of captions seemed to be flashing through Leslie's brain.

Embezzlement . . .
Murder by causing suicide . . .
False statement . . .
Adultery . . .

He must be going cranky; adultery was one of the things of which he was not guilty. Call it fornication. But fornication was not a criminal offence. Nor could he be said to have made a false statement until his passport form had been completed. And if he were to return the hundred pounds to the bank intact, as it still was, he would not be guilty of embezzlement either. That only left murder.

If only he could be sure that Lil had been quite dead when he left her, his mind would be easier; he would be relieved of murder by neglect. And as for murder by causing suicide, he could even be relieved of that because the last, the very last thing he expected, was to find that Lil, of all people, had done this thing.

Now that he had discovered by chance that he was a reasonably good salesman and could make an excellent living, far in excess of what he had made working in the bank, there was no need for the hundred pounds. All he had to do was to put it into a registered envelope and post it back. But if he posted it from London the postmark would show clearly that Leslie Williams was still in London; which was not a good thing. He would have to think up some less obvious means of getting the money back.

And that awful devil in his mind could be laid to rest once and for all, if he could only satisfy himself about Lil's death.

With his final cup of coffee, he pondered over the means of doing this: he could telephone to the flat, but if the flat had been taken over by one of Lil's relatives, which was more than likely, his voice would be recognised at once.

Or he could go and see for himself what the situation was. Which would be absurd so long as he wished to keep Leslie W. Dunright intact. And furthermore it was very much like the old saw about the dog returning to its vomit.

"Good morning, Mr. Dunright." Miss Brown, having finished her breakfast, was passing his table on her way out to her work. She bowed slightly and formally but was there a small special smile on her lips for him? He watched her trim little figure as she walked briskly out of the room. She wore mercerised stockings for work and nylons at the week-end. He knew of no other woman who wore such stockings. And yet she was not what he would call an eccentric; under the cotton stockings, she had the slimmest of ankles which were by no means flattered by the lace-up Oxfords with the medium heel; she was an individual, an independent woman who wore sensible footwear for work.

The shaking old gentleman and two of the elderly couples

were still quietly breakfasting when Miss Lyneaux bounced in like a cheerful school-girl, bursting with life and camaraderie. " Good morning all! " She sat down and ordered a large breakfast with the smug satisfaction of someone who has no need to bother about her figure.

Leslie sat and stared downwards at his coffee cup and at his own wrists, emerging thinly from his off-the-peg suit sleeves. The pulse was visible, working away furiously like the pistons of a small tug boat. Surely, he thought, it was going much too fast?

" I'll tell you what I'm going to do to-day," she cried and proceeded to do so, but Leslie was too fascinated by his pulses to listen to her; and a little refrain came to him from the days when gramophone records did not bend like cardboard and were not called discs:

> " *Why does my heart miss a beat,*
> *At the footsteps on the street ?*
> *It's that precious little thing called . . . love.*"

" Mr. Dunright, sir." Sawley was bending over him. " There's a gentleman to see you . . . a Mr. Cross."

And hot in his wake came the gentleman in person.

" 'Ullo, Les! How are you, old cock? Finished brekker? That's right; well, there's a job on."

Leslie became extremely uncomfortable. In the diningroom of the Lugano, Charlie Cross looked as out of place as a flamingo pecking with the pigeons in the Place Dauphine.

" Sh . . . sh! " Leslie hissed.

Upon which Charlie lowered his voice to a hoarse whisper, conspiratorial and infinitely suspect.

" Look," Leslie suggested irritably, " let's go out, shall we? "

Outside on the pavement, beside the mud-splashed Chevrolet, Charlie said he had come by a specially nice line in pram covers, real class.

" Oh no! Pram covers! What do you take me for? "

" Just a minute. Just a minute! Keep your hairs on, Les, such as they are! Let me show you."

"Well, for God's sake not here. Not right in front of the hotel!"

So Charlie drove round the corner, out into Cromwell Road and, with the traffic rushing past, brought out a series of small rugs of fluffy, silky material in a variety of bright colours. "What do you think of this lot?"

Leslie fingered them thoughtfully. "But pram rugs!" he said distastefully.

"Mohair!"

"Never heard of it."

"That doesn't mean it don't exist," Charlie said huffily.

"What is a mo, anyway?"

"Don't try and be funny. It's a sheep, a kind of sheep you get in the Highlands of Scotland, only these come from abroad. Beautiful, aren't they? Soft as silk, cuddly! In fact the mo lives on silkworms——" he gave a great guffaw of laughter in which Leslie did not join.

"I don't mind selling gent's shoes," he said reasonably, "and I don't mind selling silver teapots but I do draw the line at this lot."

"But they're the best of the lot! It's all the rage, this mohair. The women will fall for it like . . . you'll see! And the colours!"

Leslie shook his head firmly. "No," he declared with dignity, "there is a point beyond which I will not go."

Charlie got out a cigarette, putting his case back without offering one to Leslie. He smoked, inhaling in great gulps and tapping his thick forefinger rapidly and nervously on the steering wheel.

"Now look——" he started reasonably.

But Leslie was firm. "What do you take me for?"

Charlie snapped back: "Stubborn!"

"It's undignified."

"Undignified, selling class goods like this? You don't know what you're talking about. Blokes in the rag trade are just as much business men as anyone else. You don't catch them talking about *undignified*." He talked himself angry. "Bloody little snob!" he said finally.

Leslie was slow to anger. He had never been angry in his life, merely annoyed, and he knew not that tingling of the guts that makes the least of men strike out blindly, either verbally or in fact.

"I'm no snob," he pointed out. "If I'd been that, I'd never have stood in the market these half dozen times, selling what I have sold for you already."

"It isn't as though I was asking you to sell me a lot of bras, or rayon bloomers. When I was in the mail order business, there wasn't anythink I didn't sell. Nothink!"

"I can believe that," Leslie murmured and immediately regretted it because Charlie turned on him with an altogether savage look.

"Throw your mind back, if you please."

"What do you mean?" Leslie stammered.

"Just throw your mind back."

He let go of Leslie's wrist and took out another cigarette which he lighted from the last one. "I said no questions asked, didn't I?"

Leslie made no reply.

"Well, didn't I?"

"I don't know why you take it upon yourself to assume," and he pronounced it fastidiously, "that I should mind answering any questions whatever. In fact, I might say, you were insulting me by doing so."

"That's as maybe. But I didn't notice you seemed insulted!"

A devastating answer.

"You fell on your feet, Leslie, my boy. Oh, you're the tycoon now all right. Twenty guinea buckskin shoes and the lot. But I'll give you a for instance: you looked pretty lost, let me tell you, when you came out of the Labour Exchange that Monday morning only three and a half weeks ago." He paused. "Mr. Leslie William Dunright!" He laughed and some smoke caught him unawares so that he coughed convulsively. "Dunright!" he repeated when he had recovered sufficiently. "Funny name, isn't it? One of the Shropshire Dunrights, I take it. Well, let me tell you, old cock, you've done wrong turning down this lot."

Turned nasty! Well, they did turn nasty, that type. It was nothing to be surprised and hurt about.

"Who are you, Mr. Dunright?" he asked conversationally. "How come a decent little chap like you was spending the morning in the Labour Exchange? I'm only asking, that's all, just asking."

"Why——" his voice seemed oddly cracked. He started again. "Why can't you sell these things yourself?"

Apparently seeing that he was going to be more reasonable, Charlie threw off his unpleasantly sarcastic manner and showed himself once more the good-hearted but harassed salesman. "I've told you. Same applies now as it did then. It needs two to run a show like mine; me and my pal Perce. But Perce is laying in hospital, like I told you, and I'm up the wall. Look, don't you believe me?"

He did, and always had; that was the whole trouble.

"It's gospel truth," he swore soberly in a pious voice. "One of us picks it up and the other sells, we just about got it tied down."

"But why does it take so long for you to pick up the goods always?"

Charlie frowned deeply. "Now look; leave that side of it to me, will yer? It takes me hours to get the *pro formas* gone over and I've got to have this fast car, so we can get around. There's no need for me to tell you a darn thing; I pay you enough, when all's said and done!"

That was true, Leslie thought. It was only that this particular morning he, Leslie, was feeling that the job was unworthy of him. If he'd been asked to sell the pram-rugs yesterday, perhaps he would have felt differently about it.

"Come on . . . come on . . . I'm in a spot, I'll grant you, but I could get someone else . . . there's better fish in the sea than ever came out of it, as they say." There was a long pause, at the end of which Charlie said sulkily: "It must be yer sins catching up on yer."

I've come a long way, Leslie thought, in these three and a half weeks; a long way, and downhill all the way. Paris and the wine and olive belt were receding into the distant past.

"It don't make sense," Charlie grumbled on, "Qui'

honestly . . . have you taken to not shaving? It's beginning to notice. Or is it the lady-friend you wanted the kitty for's got a liking for hair on the face?" he leered. " Tell you what, Les old cock, you don't get nothink in this little ole life without luck. But you got to grab hold of it. Your bit o' luck was when I seen you outside the Labour Exchange. I reckon you'd of packed this up 'ere now if I hadn't happened along."

By " this " he meant a life of comparative luxury at the Hotel Lugano. " What are you out for to do in those genuine twenty guinea buckskin shoes? Marry money? Eh? Or what? "

And now Leslie knew what was happening; he was being blackmailed. He was now quite certain that he had seen Charlie Cross before and where would it be other than at the City and Suburban Bank? He was probably a customer whom he, Leslie, had served, and probably more often than once. In a week, on his stool in the bank, he had attended to hundreds of customers. To say that one was good at remembering faces in these circumstances would not be true. A worn and tattered paying-in book was a great deal more recognisable than a face. At the busiest time of day, he never raised his eyes above the customer's middle, the hands, the signatures on the cheques, the rows of figures to be quickly added up, the thousands of sterling notes to be flicked through. And all the time the waiting customer would be watching him through the grill and would know him perfectly by sight; would know his name, clearly and obviously displayed on the plastic disc: " Mr. Leslie Williams."

The customer would also know, if he were interested, that Mr. Leslie Williams had not been at his accustomed place in the bank for the past three and a half weeks. Though he would not be in a position to know that Mr. Leslie Williams had embezzled one hundred pounds from this same bank, he would know, being the inquisitive type he was, that the same Leslie Williams would not be hurrying away from a labour exchange on a Monday morning unless he had been summarily dismissed from the bank. But when he knew that Mr. Leslie Williams had become, suddenly, Mr. Leslie Dunright (and what a stupid name to choose!) he would know that

c

Williams, alias Dunright, was his thing, his chattel and someone with whom he could do anything he liked, with only a little turning of the screw.

For the present, until Leslie had time to make new plans and disappear, there was nothing whatever he could do but submit. But, he thought bitterly, how could he ever feel secure again? There was no security anywhere against meeting a customer of the City and Suburban Bank until he was dead. And as for luck, the only luck that would ever come his way was the bad kind.

"You bin friendly arsed——" Charlie said soberly, " to do me a favour. Won't do? Or will do? Make yer mind up."

Leslie nodded. " Will do."

" Right. I'll get you properly genned-up on the way."

" Half a tick." He started to get out of the car.

There was no doubt about it that Charlie tensed up. " What you going to do? " His eyes had narrowed slightly.

" Only change my shoes. I'm not standing in the market all day in these." But that slight tension he had registered in Charlie had given him hope, and was going to give him ideas.

As he hurried through the hall, past Sawley who stood respectfully aside to make way for the busy tycoon, Elizabeth came out of the dining-room and followed him upstairs.

" Darling." In the dark of the half-landing she wound her arms round his neck and kissed him envelopingly. It was not the sort of kiss from under which it was easy to slip away; he lent himself to it with some enthusiasm before disengaging with the words that a friend was waiting for him.

" See you to-night," she whispered and added, in a normal voice, " What a madly attractive man! "

It was only as he was changing his shoes that he realised she meant not Leslie Dunright but Charlie Cross.

CHAPTER VII

THE LITTLE gaily-coloured rugs were the most successful things that he had so far tried to sell; he sold out completely and, driving back in the evening with Charlie, he felt that elation which arises from having done a good day's business. They drove in silence but there was a feeling of slackened hostility between them. It was not until they were in Cromwell Road again that Leslie suggested that if his services were to be required again, would it not be possible to let him know in advance? Charlie pointed out reasonably enough that his business was largely conducted on the telephone; he never knew, from day to day, what he was going to have to sell or whether he would have anything at all. " I'll call you on the blower if you'd rather I do that," he suggested obligingly.

Leslie said he would. Charlie leaned across him to open the door. " Well, thanks, old man. I'll see you when I see you, then? "

With a number of serious problems to face Leslie hurried to his room with a quick nod to Sawley who, even though he was acting head waiter, succeeded at the same time in being a vigilant hall porter who missed no coming-in nor going-out.

The jotting of his expenses in his note-book and the counting up of the notes in his pocket showed him the astonishing fact that his present financial position was satisfactory to the extent of sixty-eight pounds ten shillings, the hotel bill having been paid up to the previous day and the hundred pounds with which he had started still quite intact. Never having been anything but a wage-earner, this was heady knowledge to Leslie; it had all been accumulated by his own efforts. As a wage-earner, money came to you whether you made any effort or not; wage-earning was simply a matter of keeping-on and keeping-on and, if one day you felt as energetic and omnipotent as Alexander the Great and the next day as ready to conquer the world as a shiftless ne'er-do-well shuffling out of Rowton House, the monthly cheque never varied.

He had taken Elizabeth out to dinner several times, had had a great many drinks at The Mermaid Bar, had won five pounds and lost six pounds on the horses, had done a little shopping.

The next thing was to buy a registered envelope and send the hundred pounds back to the bank: " From Leslie Williams." And posted at Charing Cross Post Office, S. W. 1.

This must be done without fail.

Just as he ought to have telephoned to the police without fail . . .

Then he shook himself irritably. If he was going to make any sort of success of things he would have to get over this ridiculous habit his mind had acquired of wallowing in remorse. Lil had given herself an overdose of sleeping tablets either accidentally or purposely; that she had done so as a result of his behaviour was not his fault but his misfortune. That was the way he must look at it if he were to retain any sort of sanity in the bustling world in which he now found himself. There was no room for sentimentality. *Let the dead bury their dead !* Looking at himself in the glass, he wondered where he had heard that Biblical phrase that dropped so aptly into his mind and what exactly it meant. He touched his small moustache. *Let the dead bury their dead!* Meaningless and rather nasty.

And now it was cocktail time, party time. He washed, changed his shoes and went down into the hall.

" Miss Lino's not come in yet, sir," Sawley said with low cunning and a straight face. " And I'm sorry, sir, I'm sorry about that horse."

" Oh, that's all right, Sawley," Leslie returned with the joviality of one who could afford to lose. " We can't always win, can we ? "

" I like to keep up the standard of wins," Sawley replied soberly. " I feel it's me has let the side down and not the horse."

Leslie went on to say cheerfully that there was no such thing as a dead cert, and if there were, racing wouldn't have the attraction it had; everybody liked to try their luck one time or another. To which Sawley replied that was so, but there were, on occasion, horses you knew couldn't lose unless there were unforeseen circumstances. Like this horse he was talking about. Now . . . given reasonable luck that horse couldn't lose, and by reasonable luck he meant that owing to this, or that, or the other, the horse actually started from the starting post. " It's a hundred to eight now," he said dreamily, " but when people see how it looks in the paddock there'll be a last minute rush. However——"

More was said about the horse but Leslie found his eyes wandering from Sawley back to the front door. Where was she? Why was she late? Was she, perhaps, having a drink elsewhere with someone?

" Let the dead bury their dead! " he murmured, unaccountably.

" Eh? " Sawley jumped.

" What does that quotation come from? "

Sawley shook his head sadly. " Never went to Sunday school, sir? "

Leslie admitted that he had, but had never paid much attention. At which Sawley clicked his tongue and said that his own mother and father had been Plymouth Brethren; he had been brought up on the Bible, knew it off by heart, he did. " It was when one of the disciples said to Our Lord that he would follow Him, but first let him go and bury his dead, and the Lord said unto him: ' Follow me and let the dead bury their dead.' That was the occasion, sir, in Matthew, if I'm not mistaken."

Leslie frowned.

" In other words, sir," Sawley went on, " let the dead look after themselves . . . no heel-taps, as it were. Puzzling, isn't it? "

It was indeed, puzzling.

" It was all this Bible business that got me so keen on horses," Sawley went on. " Me Dad was head gardener to a big race-horse owner with his own trainer, and when me Dad and Mum went off to their prayer meetings, I nipped out to the stables and the lads used to let me peek at the horses."

" I thought you didn't care for animals."

" Nor do I! " he declared, " I hate them, one of the brutes kicked me black and blue, from here to here," Sawley demonstrated on his thigh, " but I had a stop watch and some mornings I'd be out near the paddock and I'd time them; a hobby, like other boys train-spot. Two minutes to dinner, sir, looks like Miss Lino's staying out to-night."

Let the dead bury their dead might have been written for him and ought to have filled him with comfort.

She was not in when Sawley had locked up and retired to his tiny room in the basement. The TV room was empty and dark, everybody had gone to bed, but Leslie could not bring himself to go. He sat by the remains of the lounge fire and appeared to be reading a paper-back which he had picked out of the hotel bookcase. It was nearly midnight when she let herself in with her own latchkey. She was delighted to find him waiting for her, he did not ask where she had been but kissed her gratefully; together they went up to her room.

It took him several days to realise what had happened to him. People of his type, age and upbringing did not easily describe themselves as being " in love." For many hours he bore the fever and the fret and always avoided the word " love " He told himself that he was fascinated by her, "gone" on her, " silly " about her, but, however he might describe it there was the same squeezing of the heart, pounding of the pulses and absolute absorption in the beloved that is prevalent in a young man of twenty, normally described as being " in love."

And then he was tortured by her manner towards him, which was always slightly teasing. Her lack of curiosity, which at first had been a blessing, was now a torment; she couldn't be taking him seriously if she never wanted to know what his work was, what his married life had been like, what sort of circumstances he had lived in until they met. And how much was he yet another " affair " ?

An " affair " was all very well but not for him. He could steal a hundred pounds from his work; inform his wife that he was going to leave her; let the dead bury their dead; waste money on gambling, sell gaudy and worthless goods in the market place, but he could not make love to a fascinating woman without wanting to regularise the position and, as a widower, he was perfectly at liberty to do so.

But when he asked her if she would marry him, she hurt him infinitely by laughing. She was pleased, but how she laughed. To make up for it, however, she took him out for a long, lovely day in her little car. They drove into rural Essex and sat by a sea-lake and made love on the springy grass with the wild sea-birds watching them.

"You see," she said afterwards, tidying her copper hair, "we couldn't do that if we were married."

"Couldn't? What an extraordinary idea!"

"We wouldn't, then, if you like it better."

He didn't. He didn't understand at all.

And then, suddenly, driving home along the Cambridge by-pass, she asked him about Lil. "What was she like, I mean, *like*?"

Leslie found himself strangely wordless. He said she was pretty, liked a good time, liked going abroad and spending money. She was kind and pretty and, yes, nice. She was nice.

"And boring?"

He was shocked. "No, she was not boring, exactly."

"But not interesting?"

He wouldn't say that, either.

"She worked in a coffee bar up West. She always tried to be home when I got back from work; she used to have a warm evening meal for me most nights. She was a good girl, and clever, too."

"She was probably bored by you," Elizabeth said unexpectedly and he was deeply hurt until she stopped the car and explained to him that she hadn't meant anything; it was that sometimes married couples did get bored with each other, that's why she didn't want to marry. But Leslie could not "for the life of him" *see* that, though in his time he had known it. They drove back into London with the smallest shadow over their wonderful day.

She kept her car in a small garage built of concrete blocks which had evidently been knocked up hurriedly at some time fairly recently, in a position where a garage had never been intended, crouching beside a tall, grey brick semi-detached house. " But it's all my own," she said, " even though I have to pay two pounds a week for it; it's worth it to keep little old fatty in good condition." She patted her small stout car affectionately before locking the double doors and walking away towards Cromwell Road, with her arm in Leslie's.

" You're a dear little man and I am fond of you: I mean, I really am very fond of you but I don't *want* to get married. That's funny, isn't it? It is generally supposed that spinsters of my age are dying to get married; well, here's one who isn't. I couldn't be bothered with all the responsibility. I could never hope to replace Lil who, I can see, was devoted to you."

" I wouldn't say that; I had become a bit of a habit, I reckon."

" Oh yes, she was devoted to you. And I'm not your type."

" Oh, when people start talking about types——! "

" It's important. I'm flighty, really, the blood of the Bourbons taints me," she laughed. " But it's such a waste of a good widower; there are lots of women who would be delighted to marry you. Why pick on me? "

" Because I'm in love with you, I adore you."

" You think you do, darling. Hermione Brown is much more your dish."

" Good heavens! "

" You men . . . always rushing after the flashy sort. Hermione Brown is as good as . . . as good as—— "

" Stop it! " he cried.

" Whereas I like men, very much. I like that flashy Charlie-friend of yours."

" Women always go for his sort. Lil very much admired men like him! "

" Now, listen, darling. Let us go away together. Let's go to France in my little car and have a lovely long holiday together. And don't be squeamish, darling, let's go Dutch; I'll pay half. My dear little bank clerk . . . you're out of a job, aren't you? Anyone can see that. So can you afford to come away? "

" I could," he said cautiously.

"Come on, then," she cried. "Let's do it. Let's go right down to the Basque country; I know lots of cheap places to stay. It will be heavenly at this time of year."

Maps were brought out and a long delightful discussion took place. There was nothing else in the world he wanted to do. Paris and a job as courier through the wine and olive belt was nothing to this. The Basque country in a baby Austin with a woman who was half French and with whom he was in love; it was like a dream.

On sixty-five pounds?

Or one hundred and sixty-five pounds, if he did not return the hundred to the bank.

"I've got to get my passport fixed up," he said comfortably. "I need a new one."

And this casual normal remark fitted perfectly into the dream-like quality of the discussion of something which was never going to come off.

Whilst all this delightful planning was going on, Leslie looked occasionally at Miss Hermione Brown, sitting, as always at meals, with her head bent towards an open book. Sometimes he asked her how the new kitten was and every time she answered primly that it was quite well, thank you, and hurried away as though she had no desire to get into lengthy conversation.

The selling of another consignment of shoes brought him in fifteen pounds but most of that went on his hotel bill. He decided that, at the risk of wrecking plans for the Basque holiday, he must be honest about money.

"Listen," he began, "Elizabeth, my own darling, I don't know if I can afford this holiday but I must make it quite clear to you that I'm not going to let you pay a penny of my side of it. If I stay in London, I can either get a regular job or I may be able to make a bit more with that business friend of mine, Charlie Cross . . . a little matter of buying and selling. But I'm a pretty penniless bloke."

"So am I!" she cried cheerfully, "so am I. I've got to be very careful. Dividends always seem so tiny, don't they? I mean, quite a lot of money seems to bring in such a little, doesn't it? So if we go, we'll do everything on the cheap.

But it will be fun, my darling." And she threw her arms round his neck and kissed him, in which condition he found it hard to keep his mind on his paltry finances.

"That's why I have to fall back on old Sawley when I want some money for a spree," she added.

"You do that, too, do you?"

"Doesn't everybody? The Stock Exchange . . . horses . . . the pools; all of us want to make a little extra money, don't we? And I must say Sawley has an uncanny knack of picking winners, though on the whole, I am down in a year's mild gambling with him. But I'm surprised at you, ducky. I thought bank clerks didn't bet!"

"They don't. It's a wild streak in me, something I've always had to watch out for. I had an ancestor who was hanged for sheep-stealing in Welshpool market place."

She laughed. "Good for you!"

A little later Leslie was leaning on Sawley's desk. "You remember that horse you were telling me about yesterday?"

"That grey mare?"

"I expect so. You didn't tell me the name."

"Want to back it, sir?"

"Well——" A wildly unruly thought had entered his head. What about getting rid of that whole accursed one hundred pounds, the root of all the trouble, in One Fell Swoop?

"Still a hundred to eight, and if all goes well——" Sawley droned on and on.

To get rid of it, once and for all! To be quit of all the worry it entailed! There would be something satisfying about giving the lot to Sawley to put on a horse. Whereas to tamely post it back to the bank would be exactly what Leslie Williams would have done, to salve his conscience. But Leslie W. Dunright, lover, gadabout, *flaneur*, man of the world, would not hesitate to plank (as opposed to *put*) his last hundred pounds on a horse, guaranteed to win a race at a hundred-to-eight.

But at times Leslie Williams could not quite merge himself into Leslie W. Dunright; something further was needed to tip him over on to the wilder shores.

And that something was the most absurd, the most uncanny, the most extraordinary thing that had happened to him so far.

It was a birthday card which arrived on his thirty-ninth birthday, 6th May. It was one of the tall thin cards which were very much in vogue at the time.

"A letter for you, Mr. Dunright," Sawley said, his face completely expressionless. It was the first letter Mr. Dunright had received at the Lugano and he jumped with surprise.

"Oh, really! I have all my mail sent to my bank," he tried to say casually as he stretched out his hand for the long thin envelope.

"Your birthday, sir?" Sawley asked, still straight-faced but with a twinkle in his eye.

The twopenny stamp and the tucked-in flap made it an easy guess. Leslie nodded. He looked down at his own hands which had suddenly started to shake. Nobody, not a soul alive, knew, or could possibly know, that it was Leslie W. Dunright's birthday. His passport form, partially filled-in, was still in his breast pocket and had been since he wrote a fictitious date of his birth upon it.

"I do wish you many happy returns," Sawley said civilly. "I must see what the stars foretell for you, Sunday," he added. "They say May is unlucky but I have an idea May's a lucky month for punters."

His knees felt weak as he went into the lounge, sat down and drew out the card. Unlike most of them, it had no comic caption: a long, long colourful staircase showed the back view of a small boy toiling up. It was gay and brightly coloured and inside were the words: "A happy, happy day!"

Not a living soul . . . he mused . . . not a living soul! *Unless this was a card from the dead; but even the dear departed would not know his new name and address.* Or did he talk in his sleep?

"Do I talk in my sleep, Elizabeth?" he asked later.

"Darling, it is you who lie awake and look at me, not the other way round. If you do talk in your sleep, I've never heard you because I've been asleep myself."

"I only wondered. By the way, it's my birthday!"

"To-day? Darling, how lovely! An excuse for me to take you out to dinner, this time. Let's do something really exotic, like go to the Caprice. I've just given Sawley five pounds to put on one of his nags; I'll ask for it back and we'll have a blow out."

"No," he said moodily, "don't do that."

"Do let me!"

"Look, Elizabeth, we're well into May and wasting the best time of the year. Let's go; let's simply get a move on and go to France."

"Right, I'm ready when you are. I keep my room on here."

"I don't. I couldn't afford to. I'll tell Sawley he can let it for some weeks, shall I?"

"Do that. You'll probably be expected to give a week's notice."

So it was arranged that they would go in a week's time ... and about the passport; it would have to be Charlie Cross who would help. Charlie would know a quick, slick way of getting a fake passport "and no questions arsed." Soon he would ask him to help, but for the moment he had the half-completed form, and, of course, the photographs.

There was an extra photograph. "Would you like this?" Leslie asked Elizabeth casually. She took it and studied it for a minute. "Not bad as passport photographs go. You're not a bad-looking little fellow, are you? I'll wear it next my heart and sleep with it under my pillow." She tucked it away in her handbag.

"It's no good pretending we're going away separately," Elizabeth declared unexpectedly, "so I'll agree to be engaged, if you don't hold me to it. Sawley will be less shocked, that way."

Soberly Sawley accepted the fact; soberly he congratulated them. And later still, when Elizabeth had gone upstairs, Leslie, acting under the compulsion of the receipt of the birthday card, gave Sawley the packet of twenty five-pound notes he had taken from the bank. "Put the lot on that horse you've been boasting about," he said abruptly.

Sawley was shocked. "Sir! Now, sir, far be it from me———"

"Take it, man, take it," Leslie said impatiently and went out on to the front doorstep to look at the weather.

The birthday card was ominous, a warning. His mind became the consistency of jelly when he tried to discover who had sent it; he was in a kind of morbid panic when he gave the money to the hall porter, but the immediate effect of the action was one of relief. It was an unthinking, almost instinctive move of self-preservation.

One, or better still, two more days selling for Charlie Cross and he would be in a good enough financial position for the holiday, provided they really did stay in cheap places. And thinking of Charlie, he made a big effort to imagine Charlie buying the birthday card. This particular type of card was what Charlie would call class goods. He had seen them displayed in Harrods and this one would have cost one shilling and ninepence.

If, as he suspected, Charlie recognised him as a fugitive from the City and Suburban Bank, he was the only living soul who would know that Mr. Leslie Williams was Mr. Leslie Dunright. But he would not know the date of Williams's birthday and if, by some fantastic chance, he did, he would never think of sending him a birthday card. It was not the sort of thing one man did to another, and certainly no man of Charlie's type. His imagination boggled at the thought of Charlie entering a large store and choosing a one-and-ninepenny birthday card to send to him, or to anyone else.

The sending of the birthday card was essentially a female action; it was within the bounds of possibility that one of Lil's numerous female relations, most of whom disliked him and with whom he had nothing whatever in common, had remembered the date of his birthday and had sent the card spitefully, as a subtle warning that Mr. Leslie Williams was catching up on Mr. Leslie Dunright; in other words, that the police were on his track.

Standing on the top step, hands in his pockets, he felt immensely cold. There was plenty of warmth in the May sunshine but the cold Leslie felt came from within and was the same sort of coldness he had felt when he had found Lil dead lying on her bed. It was a coldness round the back of his neck, making his hair feel too short and giving him acute gooseflesh of the skin under his shirt sleeves.

"Sawley——?" he heard a gentle voice behind him. The front doors had been temporarily hooked wide open to admit the fresh spring air and Sawley was in his cubby hole, glasses on the end of his nose, the sporting page open in front of him.

"Yes, miss?"

"I'm so sorry but my sash cord has gone!"

"Not again!"

"Oh, Sawley. You say that every time!"

"But I don't know what you do with your sash cords, Miss Brown, reely I don't! Every six months, regular, one or other of them goes."

"But Sawley . . . you've said yourself . . . sash ropes aren't what they were. Cheap materials, you said. And in this London atmosphere they rot!"

Miss Brown had the single room over the front door, a slip of a narrow room with a huge sash window reaching almost to the ground, overlooking the street and giving on to the lead-covered top of the immense front portico, which area she called her balcony.

"All right, miss," Sawley said patiently, "I'll have it seen to."

"Please do. You see, in this lovely weather, I lift out my deck chair and sit on my own private balcony; and it is the bottom window that has gone. So until it is mended, I can't do that any longer."

"Leave it to me, miss."

With murmured thanks Miss Brown came out on to the top step; she was dressed in the neat suit she wore for work and had a book tucked under her arm.

"Good morning, Mr. Dunright. Isn't it a heavenly day?"

Was it? "I thought it looked like rain."

Miss Brown paused looking at him thoughtfully, "Are you all right, Mr. Dunright?"

" A bit chilly! "

" Chilly, on a lovely morning like this! "

" How is your little cat? "

Miss Brown leaned over the balustrade and looked down into the area. " Quite happy, thank you. She's not there at the moment. That other little cat, the one who disappeared so mysteriously, used to climb up on to my balcony. Look, up that drain pipe and along that ledge. I'm training this new little creature to do the same."

Leslie looked at the cat's route doubtfully. " Did it now? That was quite a brave climb."

" But she was a brave little cat! " A moment's silence and she continued. " Sawley doesn't really like me, I'm afraid. I know he's a nice obliging man, but I'm afraid I've annoyed him with my cats." She paused again. " There was such a bang this morning when I was raising my lower window. I knew at once what it was; it happens regularly. It was the weight dropping with what my father used to call ' a sickening thud'."

" I heard you asking Sawley to have it mended."

" He will, in due course, but I'll have to ask him many more times." It was said wistfully rather than complainingly. Leslie dragged his thoughts away from their own depressed area.

" And in the meantime you'll be missing all the lovely spring sunshine; on your own private balcony! "

" Never mind," she said, glancing at her watch. " I must be on my way. I shall go and sit in the park and have my sandwiches out of doors to-day, if it doesn't rain, as you think it may."

She started down the steps.

" Look," Leslie said in sudden impulse. " If you have a screwdriver and get me a length of rope, I'll fix that sash for you in a jiffy."

" Oh, thank you, Mr. Dunright. How very kind! I have a screwdriver."

" Only get the rope quickly! "

" I will indeed."

" Because I . . . we . . . that is . . . we are going away."

" Going away ? "

" Miss Lyneaux and I are thinking of getting married. As a matter of fact, we're engaged! "

She twittered with pleasure.

" We're neither of us exactly chickens so we feel rather . . . what shall I say . . . rather as though we wanted to keep it dark, for a bit anyway."

" When are you thinking of going away ? "

" In a day or so. Elizabeth has been very lucky about getting the car-passage booked; but it is easier at this time of the year."

Having indicated her pleasure, she reverted to her gently formal, slightly impersonal manner.

Leslie himself was slightly shocked that they should be going away together unmarried, but he adopted the unquestioning manner of the people with whom he now associated, who, it seemed, were not so easily shocked.

" Then I'll buy a piece of strong sash cord to-day," she stated practically. " Sawley has so much responsibility with the management away, I'm sure he'll be delighted to have one thing less to think about. I must run. Bye-bye, Mr. Dunright, for now! "

Hatless, her hair piled up, away from the jutting line of her cheek and chin, tiny in her sensible laced-up Oxfords, she walked away down the street. There was no possible chance of her looking back and waving cheerfully before stepping off the pavement. Self-contained, contented and yet by no means unobservant: he liked her. But to call her his " dish " was the sort of absurd exaggeration with which his darling Elizabeth larded her conversation.

And now he heard the voice of his beloved.

" Sawley, my pet. That fiver I gave you last night."

" Want it back, miss ? "

" How did you guess ? " Pause. " Thanks. I know I'm a ghastly nuisance but I want this to celebrate Mr. Dunright's birthday."

" That's all right, miss. Thinking none of that blood's been much good when it comes to a struggle and, looking at to-day's field, maybe it's as well."

She laughed. "We'll eat the fiver, instead of giving it to the bookie. It's lucky you hadn't put it on already."

"I left it till to-day on purpose——" There was more he wanted to tell her about horseflesh but Elizabeth did not want to hear. She joined Leslie on the doorstep.

"Dinner to-night, then? It's a date. Now look, darling, I'm going to spend to-day getting the car gone over. And I'm going to get some of the sort of spare parts we can take with us: petrol pump, fan belt, can you think of any other vital thing we ought to have?"

But Leslie did not know anything about cars so she said she would go round and have a talk to the people who maintained her car.

He waited around until such time as was too late for Charlie Cross to telephone or to come and then, carrying the long narrow slip of cold terror that was his birthday card in his breast pocket, he did a number of ordinary things; bought himself a new pair of bathing shorts, a road map of the Basque country, and a bottle of after-shave lotion. And now he knew he should be attending to the question of his passport but once more he stuffed the knowledge away like a dirty shirt that he could not, at the moment, be bothered to wash.

But when he was walking round the underground waiting hall of Piccadilly Circus, with the shop windows and the kiosks, and the dozens of people waiting for other people, he suffered a few minutes of panic which, later, he called "an attack of nerves." All his newly-found confidence deserted him. Approaching the Lower Regent Street exit from the station on his way to Lillywhites for a dashing "sports shirt," he was lifting his foot to place it on the bottom step when a wave of terror shook him. He stood still whilst impatient people brushed hurriedly past him. He could not, he utterly could not, mount the stairs and go out into the Circus. Down in the station he was safe, anonymous: outside there were policemen, people who knew him both as Leslie Williams and Leslie Dunright; outside was Lil's world, Elizabeth's world, Charlie Cross's world. Down here he was nobody and there was no need to act, to watch his step, to take care, to invent, to dissemble, to remember, to lie. His new personality had grown up too fast around him. Too quickly it had brought new responsibilities, when all he had wanted was to be alone with the pigeons in the Place Dauphine.

He was frightened; he was deathly frightened. Because something was going to happen. No sort of happy life could be built up on the ghastly wreck of his married life with Lil and he was mad ever to have thought it could.

Whilst all this was tearing his mind to shreds he was walking round and round the station with the purposeless haste of people exercising round the deck of a ship. After half an hour of it, he was in what Sawley would have called a " muck sweat." He stopped by the sweet kiosk and brought out the card. " A happy, happy day! " No signature. The address on the envelope was typed: it would be! The stamp stuck on carefully and straight. The postmark: London, S.W.1, 6.15 p.m. 5th May. Putting both card and envelope together he tore them across, and across, and across. Then it was too thick to tear; he halved it, and tore it across and across; then the other half, across and across. There was a litter bin nearby. Holding his hand over it he let the small fragments drop slowly into it, a few at a time. Then walking over to another he did the same, and again, until there were no torn scraps left in his hands.

Anyone watching him would have thought him mad. But nobody in this particular place watched anybody else's movements; other people were too concerned with their own affairs.

Somewhat relieved of his neurosis, he mounted the stairs and came out into the sunshine. A few steps farther and he was in the store.

" I want a sports shirt, please. Something gay. Yes, for beach wear."

CHAPTER VIII

FROM THEN ON, the sequence of events had to be recapitulated and, looking back, it would seem that everything that happened was significant in that it formed a pattern; his movements had a deadly precision so that, finally, they were seen to dovetail, showing an evil perfection. Looking back, it was terrifying to find that disaster hung and depended upon the most tenuous, insignificant details: the decision to have the birthday dinner at a small Soho restaurant; a broken sash cord; a run-down battery.

They had the birthday dinner at a little French restaurant in Soho because Elizabeth had found she must spend so much on the spare parts for her car and the work the mechanic was to do on it before it was ready to go abroad, that she felt the original idea of dinner at the Caprice was too extravagant. If, however, they had gone there, they would not have had so much wine and, if they had not had a second bottle of excellent hock, Leslie would not have been so madly indiscreet as to talk about the hundred pounds he had given to Sawley to put on a horse.

The people at the next table were talking about money. "It's funny," Elizabeth remarked, "whenever you overhear scraps of other people's conversation, they always seem to be talking about money, don't they?"

"But of course. You can't do anything without money."

Elizabeth laughed, as she so often did inexplicably. "That's one of your super-trite remarks," she jeered gently. She smiled and put out her hand to cover his as she said it, but nevertheless it stung.

He said carelessly: "Well, I've put a hundred pounds on one of Sawley's 'dead certs'."

She gasped. "Leslie! How could you?"

"In cash," he went on proudly. "I had the notes on me, proceeds from the sale of a few oddments that belonged to my late wife. It was a nest-egg. I was keeping it for a rainy day.

But I've staked the lot and if I win we won't need to go away for a *Dutch* treat, as you call it!" He drank another glass of wine, enjoying the impression that he had undoubtedly made. " *I* shall pay."

She looked completely bewildered. " You're such a strange little man," she said, shaking her head, " I suppose that is why I'm fond of you. So conventional, so typical, and yet capable of sudden impulsive action that knocks one sideways with astonishment."

" That sheep-stealing ancestor," he returned smugly, dabbing the traces of red wine from the corner of his mouth with the paper napkin.

" That little moustache you have sprouted makes you look even more everybody's idea of the decent-living, absolutely predictable, middle-class Englishman. And yet . . . and yet, you can do a damn' silly thing like that! "

" Now I've shocked you," he said, satisfied. " You have always been the one to shock up to now. And you always say that people who are shocked are those who need shocking. So you see! "

" See what? "

" That you shock me by what you say and I shock you by what I do. So we're quits."

" But a hundred pounds! When did you give it to him? "

" This morning."

" And for what race? "

" Oh, I dunno. He talks so much and so knowledgeably; I don't pay attention half the time."

" What horse? "

" Dunno that, either."

" I sometimes wonder about Sawley, but whenever I start wondering, he comes across with a win. So I grab it and leave it at that. But when it comes to putting a hundred pounds in his hands, you ought to know something about the horse, and the race and the odds."

" But the whole thing is done on a friendly basis. Look how obligingly he handed back the fiver to you to-day! "

" Oh, I know, but oh, great glory! How did you ever come to give him a whole hundred pounds? "

"Never mind," he returned comfortably, "I've just about got enough to pay my way and when we get back from France I'm going to get down to it."

"To what?"

"To regular earning again."

But she was still thinking about the hundred pounds. It was fading daylight when they came out; an evening with magic in it, the sky losing its light and becoming a pure dark blue and the lights of Piccadilly Circus as bright and fresh as though they had come on to-night for the first time.

Arm-in-arm they walked through the underground station on their way to the escalator and Leslie, happy, full of wine, and now strangely self-satisfied, did not give the smallest thought to the hunted, haunted creature with a nervous crisis who had, a few hours previously, dropped numerous scraps of paper into the litter bins.

As they approached the Lugano, she said that it would have been nice to go for a short run in the car to Hampstead Heath for some fresher air but she had been obliged to leave the battery at the service station to be charged.

Then Leslie, looking up at the great portico, was reminded of the window above it and said that he had promised Miss Brown he would mend her sash cord, if she had remembered to buy one.

"Poor little Hermione; you go and do her window, by all means. Are you a handy man, then?"

"I can change a sash cord, I hope."

"But not tinker with cars?"

He found that slightly mocking air alternately stimulating and irritating.

"Not cars . . . women," he flashed back and left her, as he remembered later, "in stitches."

There is a difference between sash windows in Ealing and those in Cromwell Road, which is mainly size. With Miss Brown in admiring attendance, he lifted out the lower sash but it was much heavier than he had expected; he could hardly get a strong enough grip with his arms stretched as widely as in crucifixion and was obliged to ask her to take one end of it. The fixing of the pulley and rope went splendidly but when it came to lifting the sash back, he caught her eye. She said: "You can't manage it, you know, Mr. Dunright. It needs two, really it does."

"I'll ask Sawley to help."

"He usually takes an hour off about this time for his evening drink."

"It's past ten o'clock. He'll be back, surely."

She hesitated. "He'll be annoyed, you know."

"Does it matter?"

"I don't like annoying Sawley. He's such a dear, really, and looks after us all like a guardian angel. But I know I annoy him because of my cats. And now he'll realise that I didn't wait for him to get the window fixed, he'll be even more irritated with me."

"We'll ask What'sit," Leslie suggested.

"You mean Mr. Thingummy, the scientist, with the awful German name?"

Leslie nodded. "He usually retires early to his room and his books, doesn't he?"

After further discussion, the physicist was approached by Miss Brown, with a gentle tap on his door: "Oh, I wonder if you would be good enough to give Mr. Dunright a hand with my window?"

Infinitely bored by the necessity of associating with lunatics but polite in every circumstance the young man obliged. It was now quite dark and the light from the window of her room showed clearly to Sawley, on his way back from his evening drink at the Double Gloucester, what was happening. He arrived on the scene just as the window was being opened and shut in a final testing.

"What's goin' on 'ere?" he asked in the manner of the headmaster catching the dorm in the middle of a pillow fight.

"Oh, Mr. Sawley, you are so frightfully busy these days, I thought I would relieve you of having to do this. Mr. Dunright and Mr. . . . er very kindly helped me."

Frowning deeply, the hall porter looked round Miss Brown's room for any signs of cat. But she had been too clever to leave traces about. Finally he looked at Leslie.

His look said a number of things. Leslie had always been aware that Sawley eyed him with suspicion which, in the weeks he had spent at the Lugano had, he thought, been assuaged. But here it was renewed in double strength and he felt it blowing coldly round him: a quick-worker, this Mr. Dunright; quite one with the ladies; first Miss Lino, and now Miss Brown; flashy American cars, phoney young men, bundles of five-pound notes thrown casually about! He was somebody to be watched, and watched carefully. He, Sawley, was not going to allow any unpleasant happenings at the Lugano with the management away, not if it could be avoided. Nylon stranglers and con-men were thick on the ground in South Ken these days but the Lugano had always kept aloof from that sort of thing; the hotel had a very high standard of morality and a fine record, nothing untoward was going to happen under Sawley's supervision, not if he could help it. Granted it had been he, Sawley, who had practically invited Mr. Dunright in; it may be that this very fact was now causing him to be unduly suspicious. Mr. Dunright had not developed in accordance with his gentlemanly looks; not by a long way. These con-men were always smooth; invariably a success with the ladies; usually wore that faintly helpless air.

"I had already made arrangements to have that job done yesterday," the "sir" was a little delayed.

"I'm sorry, Mr. Sawley," Miss Brown said briskly, "I really was trying to help, you know."

Sawley, acting under provocation, refrained from telling them to "break it up" but his manner left them in no doubt that he was deeply injured.

Miss Brown suddenly "broke it up" in her own inimitable way: without a smile or a vestige of what is usually called charm, she got the three men out of her room not at the drop of a hat but at the tiny sound, which she prayed that only she heard, of a miaow. It came from the depths of her closed wardrobe.

The next day started, as so many days at the Lugano began, with a mild argument about the weather. This took place after breakfast, on the front doorstep, under the portico. One old gentleman, newspaper tucked under his arm, said that it looked like rain, and another old gentleman, also carrying a newspaper under his arm, said he was mistaken, that faint fog was not a sign of rain but of a beautiful day. A third old gentleman said that the wireless said the day would start well but by evening there would be scattered showers. The first old gentleman said he still thought it looked like rain and stumped indoors. Sawley, at his desk, was holding forth about the prospects for the racing somewhere or other and that if it rained the course would be less perfect and would make a big difference to the horse of the day. Leslie wondered if that would be the horse that would carry his money, but felt that after last night's scene in Miss Brown's room, he would allow Sawley time to get over it before having any more conversation.

Miss Brown had already gone to work and now Elizabeth came out, wearing a crisp black linen frock and carrying white gloves and a white bag.

"How nice you look," he said approvingly. "Having lunch with an admirer?"

"An old aunt at Harrods," she answered. "The English one. She'd have kittens if she knew I was going away with you." She came close to him. "Darling, did you have a happy day?"

He jumped and a cold shiver ran through him.

"I mean yesterday, your birthday."

"Yes, of course." He recovered himself quickly, smiled and added: "And a happy, happy night."

She smiled and then clapped her gloved hand to her mouth: "Oh, damn! I've remembered something! The old battery the garage have put me in is in pretty poor condition. Would you come and start the car for me by hand, darling?"

"Of course, of course!"

As they walked along to the garage, she asked if to-day was the day of the race on which he had staked all that money. He said he wasn't sure and she said she did not know how he could bear the suspense. Why didn't he ask Sawley? But he said he would rather not know; it would make an anxiety on a lovely day when he hadn't a trouble in the world and he pressed her arm close to his side.

She unlocked the garage with the key from her handbag and found the starting handle, in a plastic case in the back of the car. " It's never been used," she said. " I'll get in and make sure the gear is in neutral and you shove this handle into the hole in the front and wind, only keep your thumb out of the way! "

Three pulls and the car had started. She put her head through the window. " Clever boy! Come and kiss me."

This over, she said that she had half-a-mind to take him along to Harrods " to see what Auntie would say if I said we are engaged! " and laughed at his shocked expression. She backed the car out, he threw down the starting handle, locked the doors and gave her the key.

" I'll run you back to the hotel." It was a matter of three hundred yards or so; he said he would enjoy the walk. She said in that case she would get on as she had quite a busy day, what with one thing and another. He told her to take care of herself and kissed her once more. She laughed and handed him her pocket handkerchief to wipe the lipstick off his mouth. Blushing slightly, he did this and gave it back to her.

" See you to-night," she said and, with a wave of her immaculate glove, and a frisky burst of sound from the exhaust, drove off.

As soon as he turned the corner out of Cromwell Road, he saw the large dirty pale blue car with Charlie Cross leaning against it, his feet on the pavement, in the relaxed attitude of one who has everything perfectly under control, and always will have. He was smoking and raised a languid hand as Leslie approached.

" I know you like variety," he greeted him, " but you played up somethink shocking over those coloured pram rugs. I'm putting you back on suède shoes, chum. Lovely spring weather," he pronounced it " wevver," " and you'll sell out quicker 'un you was selling hot cakes, the lot. Cor! What a dew-drop of a day, eh? "

Knowing, on the old principle of the cussedness of things that, if he put on his old shoes in preparation, Charlie would not come, he had put on his best suède shoes. He had badly wanted Charlie to come, partly because he now needed the money, and partly because he did not like the thought of another idle day.

Charlie, always very *au fait*, glanced at his shoes. " Goin' in to change? Righty-ho. Make it snappy! "

As he mounted the steps, Leslie could have sworn he saw the back of Sawley's head disappearing into the shadows of the kitchen regions. He changed his shoes and when he came down again, Sawley's cubby hole was still deserted; it was unusual for him to be absent when the doors were hooked wide open. He was deliberately avoiding him.

Back in the market place, Leslie arranged his stock in the manner of one born to it. He felt a definite pride and pleasure in what he was doing. Several stall holders, as well as Mrs. State, nodded to him; he was one of them. He began selling with that jaunty air which he so admired in some other salesmen who had to get rid of their goods in a day. When the market superintendent approached, Leslie greeted him like an old friend, though the superintendent himself was less enthusiastic.

But nevertheless, whatever happened, whether Elizabeth and he married, or whether they decided, after the holiday, that they would be happier not married to each other, this was his last, positively his last day, selling in a market place. The few times he had sold had helped to make Leslie Dunright, that nonentity, into an entity. It had now served its purpose and was finished ... done ... over. If Elizabeth knew what he did for a living, it would be the end. Oh, she was free and easy enough but she had very definite ideas about class, and selling in an open market put him right out of any class whatever with which Elizabeth would have dealings, social or amatory. She may have been amusing about Charlie Cross but that was as far as it would go. She might even be playfully flirtatious but if once she knew that he was a glorified barrow-boy, the whole subject of Charlie Cross would become one immense joke to be giggled over and made fun of for a long time.

" Sold right out? Leslie, the super-salesman," Charlie

greeted him cheerfully in the late afternoon, coming up suddenly as Leslie was tying the empty boxes into bundles for scrap.

Going back in the car, Leslie brought out the proposition which he had been turning over for some time in his mind. But first he told Charlie that this was the last time he would be selling for him in the market.

" For Christ's sake, why? " Charlie snarled and Leslie winced.

" Don't swear like that. There's no need for it," he said uncomfortably.

" Pardon. But isn't there just! That's left me in a proper jam! "

" What about your friend Perce? How is he getting on? He should be around shortly, shouldn't he? "

" Perce? Oh, he'll live okay. He's as keen to get back to it as I am. But it's complete rest, laying in bed, for him for weeks' and further weeks' convalescence—eight to ten bloomin' weeks before he'll be back. And when he gets back on his legs, he'll have to do the driving; they won't let him stand all day, too tiring."

" Well, I'm off to France at the week-end."

" Strike a light! "

" For four weeks."

" Cor, strike me peculiar! "

" So I shan't be available."

There was a long unhappy silence spiced occasionally with a picturesque expletive.

" Can't you get your friend Perce's wife back from the West country? " Leslie suggested, helpfully.

" His what? " Charlie cupped his ear in order to hear above the noise of the traffic jam of which they were part.

" His wife! " Leslie yelled.

" Oh, his wife." Charlie stroked his chin thoughtfully. " Cor," he said at last, " you haven't half balled-up the works! "

He was common, Leslie thought. Quite definitely common.

There was another long pause in the conversation. Whilst Charlie manœuvred the great pale blue hull quite skilfully, threading his way in and out of traffic as easily as though his car were no bigger than Elizabeth's baby Austin, he was thinking. The result was that, when they had reached the Law Courts end of the Strand, he drew into the indentation in the kerb, beside the Wine Lodge lamp post, where it is possible to park for a few minutes, and suggested they go in for a drink. " A short one, eh? All the business dealings you and me've had and never a quickie together," he pleaded.

Leslie gave the suggestion a moment's cautious thought and, seeing nothing against it, agreed. He had had nothing to eat other than a rather nasty meat pie with Mother State's usual cup of tea, and a bar of chocolate. Inside the Wine Lodge, Charlie, without asking him, ordered him a large dark sherry-and-gin and a large pale sherry-and-gin for himself. The next round Charlie ordered two more of the same. The third round they were both back on plain sherry because Charlie was fussy about drink when he was driving. He never touched a drop when he was driving, he said, emptying his second gin-and-sherry down his throat and adding that this particular mixture anæsthetised his tonsils and that's why he drank it: " Kills all the germs you pick up during the day." He lit a cigarette and looked speculatively at Leslie to see what effect the drink was having on him but all that happened was that Leslie said his late wife used to like gin-and-sherry, a dull remark which did not require an answer.

It was only when they were back in the car that the drink began to give him a feeling of wisdom, patience, experience of the world and a profound knowledge of the ways of men. " You remember," he started, " when we first met you said that with my looks and your brain we might get somewhere in partnership? "

" Um."

" Well, it's like this. I was wondering if, when I get back from France, I could set up in a mail order business, with your help."

Charlie gave a yelp of laughter and continued to laugh. He laughed so much that he choked and was obliged to slow the car down to walking pace. " Oh dear me! "

Leslie felt considerably irritated.

"Cut it out," he grumbled, "it's not all that funny!"

"Oh, Leslie boy, you'll be the death of me; honest, you'll kill me."

"I might," he agreed huffily.

"You may remember that, at the same time, upon that memorable occasion if I remember right, I told you I didn't trust you no farther than I could kick you."

But Leslie had been a humbled, badly frightened little man in those far off days four weeks ago. He said nothing, remembering himself as he had been.

"Leslie, old chum, anybody can't start up a mail order business, just like that. Everything's got to be——" Charlie raised his hand from the driving wheel and pointed his thumb and first finger daintily together ". . . just so. They watch you like an 'ork! Protecting the public, they call it, and they're right, too. If the public haven't got confidence in ordering goods they haven't seen by post, the mail order business wouldn't exist any more. What an idea!"

But the gin-and-sherry in his empty stomach, now far from making him more good-humoured, was beginning to cause Leslie to feel something which he had never felt in his life: anger.

"I don't know what makes you say that," he returned, tight-lipped. "You're insulting, that's what you are, insulting!"

The alcohol was having the opposite effect on Charlie; he was more tolerant, relaxed, good-humoured.

"Come off of it, boy!" Charlie begged. "Folk in glass houses shouldn't throw stones, as they say. There's none of us is exactly a lily-white boy. We've all got something we don't want known. Some of us more and some of us less. If you're really serious about that mail order idea, we could have a talk about it when you get back from Lar Belle Fronce. Have you got a passport, by the by?"

"Of course!" Leslie's face was contorted by the strength of his thoughts. "Everything about me is open and above board, I'd like you to know. There's nothing I wouldn't like known!"

"Keep yer hair on, I never said there was."

"But you've implied it; you imply it all the time."

"Honest to God, I've not!"

"If you think I resemble somebody you've . . . you've met before . . . then think again. Mistakes have been made in the past . . . mistakes in identity are always being made."

They were going through Sloane Square. Charlie now stopped the car by the kerb and turned, with some curiosity, to look at Leslie.

"Here, cool off," he suggested. "That drink's done you no good, no good at all."

Leslie glared at him angrily.

"We've got on marvellous to date, you and me," Charlie went on placatingly. "No need to tear it all up because you've had some drink you're not used to."

"It's not that, it's that you're so damned insulting."

"Listen, chum. I never saw Leslie W. Dunright before, I swear it."

Leslie found he was breathing heavily. He listened to his own breathing for a moment in surprise. Then he said: "Before what?"

"I never knew you before."

"Then what right have you to imply, to imply that there's something shady, something shady——" Leslie began stammering with the flux of emotion with which he was overcome.

Using the deep voice which he assumed on solemn occasions, Charlie held up his hand, as though swearing in a witness box with a bible in that same hand. The dropping of his aitches was patchy. "I know nothing whatever against Mr. Leslie Dunright," he declared formally. "I've always been very pleased with what you've done for me and our business dealings have been perfectly happy. I sincerely hope," he added piously, "that in the future they will continue to run as smooth as in the past, so help me God."

Leslie was beginning to feel sick. He got out of the car. "I'll walk the rest of the way."

Charlie held out his hand. "I'll see you when I see you, then?"

"I don't know if I'll come back to the Lugano after France,

but if I don't, they'll have my address." He ignored the outstretched hand but only because he was feeling very sick now.

"And phone number so's I can get you on the blower, eh?"

But a spasm of annoyance now crossed Charlie's face. "And as I say," he went on with a curious look at Leslie, "you don't have to worry too much becos I got nothink against Mr. Leslie Dunright!" He slammed the door of the car, the window was lowered and Leslie quite distinctly heard him say, before he shot away from the kerb, "Nothing whatever against Mr. Leslie Dunright."

The repetition of the name sounded, to say the least of it, strange. Leslie managed to cross to the island and convey himself down the steps of the public lavatory, where he was very sick.

CHAPTER IX

IT WAS AFTER eight o'clock when he got back to the Lugano. Dinner over, Sawley was in the dining-room, clearing away and the residents were having coffee in the lounge. He did not want any dinner. He went upstairs, took off his outer clothes and lay down on the bed, which had already been turned down for the night; he felt cold and was shaking as though with an ague.

He lay for a long time, listening to the noise of the traffic along Cromwell Road, then he fell asleep.

He had a strange, horribly confused dream, in which Elizabeth and Lil were one person; one moment she was Lil and the next moment she was Elizabeth and he was arguing with them both. He didn't know what he was arguing about but the outcome was terribly important, and both the women were laughing at him; they threw back their heads and he saw all their fine strong teeth and their pink tongues and they laughed and laughed. He woke with a jerk and he was crying as he had not cried since his mother died.

A nightmare, that was it! He'd often had nightmares as a child and his mother had always run to him to comfort him.

Now there was no Mum, no Lil. Only Elizabeth. He must go and be comforted.

It was dark now, his watch said eleven-thirty. He got up and splashed cold water over his face, dressed, combed his hair, took an Alka-Seltzer, cleaned his nails and then, opening his door slightly, he listened.

There was absolute silence in the house. The staircase lights were left on all night, with low-burning bulbs. He went along to Elizabeth's room, past all the pairs of shoes that stood outside the doors like mongrel watchdogs.

Without knocking he opened her door, went in, closed the door behind him and tiptoed across to the bed. The curtains were drawn for the night as they always were by the visiting chambermaid. He was strongly reminded of another occasion when he had tiptoed across a darkened bedroom, with a still figure in the bed. But at once it was clear from the light from the street lamp shining through the space above the curtains and reflected from the ceiling, that nobody was in the bed.

So that was that! He shut the door quietly behind him and made his way downstairs.

He turned on the light in the lounge and sat in an armchair moodily, biting at a fragment of loose skin at the side of his thumb nail.

As a whole, the sex were not to be trusted, that was the long and the short of it. Elizabeth's faintly mocking air had always been an embarrassment to him; but she had always been perfectly frank about liking men, he had to admit that.

There had even been times, on their foreign holidays, for instance, when he had thought even Lil a bit too fond of getting into conversation with strange men. She, too, was one who clearly liked men but, in her case, he had closed his mind to this fact. There were times when he had had to rebuke her, as when she rolled her eyes and said: " Ooh, a lovely man! " and certain occasions when she winked quite saucily. Once he had even gone so far as to tell her that she was so ladylike in the ordinary way, he didn't know how she could wink like that.

Elizabeth, now, was a great deal more ladylike than Lil; she was, and he was proud of it, a real lady. He loved her in a way he failed to remember having loved Lil and he had been sure, quite sure, that for the moment, anyway, she loved him in her way.

For an hour or more he sat and meditated upon the mutability of female affairs and suddenly realised with a shock that it was a quarter to one.

And there was Sawley, an unfamiliar Sawley, unshaven and undistinguished, wearing over striped pyjamas, an old woollen cardigan with long, almost trailing corners on either side, in which were situated the sagging pockets which had clearly been used for many years to carry a great many heavy things. A Sawley risen from sleep with pillow-tousled hair and dream-clouded eyes but making an effort to be brisk.

"Oh, it's you, Mr. Dunright. How did you get in, sir?"

"I haven't been out, Sawley. I've been sitting here in the lounge, look, the light's on!" And why not? was implied.

"Waiting for Miss Lino? I see. That's all right, then. Miss Lino has her own key."

"I know she has."

Sawley gave him a look which plainly said: "Why stay up, then?" But he said: "Right you are, then. I'll leave you to put out the lounge light when you turn in, sir? G'night."

Which clearly showed that in Sawley's opinion Miss Lyneaux's staying out late was no unusual event. Leslie turned out the light and went up to bed.

"There's a nasty little east wind sprung up," one old gentleman said with a shiver; "I don't think I'll go for my usual toddle round the Serpentine to-day."

"Nonsense, we're going through a warm spell!" another old gentleman contradicted him. "The wireless said last night it would be warm to-day; just the day for a stroll in the park, what?"

"Look at all that wastepaper blowing along!" the first old gentleman said testily. "You can see at a glance it's a nasty cold wind." He hurried indoors so that he could not be contradicted again and left the second old gentleman smiling sheepishly at Leslie and saying: "He couldn't be more wrong, poor old chap."

Sawley came through the front door with a bustling worried look on his face. "The chambermaid tells me Miss Lino never got home last night, sir," he told Leslie in a low voice. "Did you know she was staying out for the night?"

"No, I didn't!"

"She never left no message . . . it's very unlike her. I wondered if you'd be good enough, sir, to go along and see if her car is back as usual, in her garage."

Leslie said he would certainly do that. But what about the garage key? Sawley said that she would have the key with her but that by going round the side he would find a small window; he, Sawley, passed the garage almost daily; he knew she always closed the doors and left them locked when she was out in the car. If Mr. Dunright looked through the window he would be able to see if the car was put away. "If not," Sawley shook his head, concerned, "it's my guess she's had a nasty accident!"

"Lord, I hope not!"

"Well, I mean to say, Miss Lino's not one to stay out without letting any of us know. Most particular that way, she is."

To get to the garage, it was necessary to cross Cromwell Road, walk the length of a block and turn down a street with shops. The garage was a few steps down the street, where the houses had not yet become shops, up a short gravelly drive with the old scraggy laurel, black with soot, a wispy privet, and an enthusiastic, but dirty lilac, now in bloom. Lilacs are trees to gladden the heart but when they grow in Earl's Court they have the opposite effect, engendering in the sensitive as much depression as an over-dressy hat. Pushing past the lilac, Leslie looked in at the tiny, higher than breast-high window. He could see nothing but his own anxious face. He made a visor for his eyes with his two hands and, peering through, with his hands against the glass, he was able to see the roof of the small car. He gave the garage doors a pull, to see if they would open, but they were locked with the Yale lock. He walked down the street to the shops. There was a small group of all the usual shops, greengrocer, grocer, butcher, ironmonger, and a tobacconist and newsagents', where he got some cigarettes. It was the newsagents' to which he had always been for his morning papers.

But back at the hotel, Sawley had a further practical suggestion. He would ring up her auntie, an old lady he knew well by sight, and Miss Lino's nearest relation in London. He was sure there would be quite a simple explanation. Maybe the old lady had been taken ill and Miss Lino had stayed with her and had not yet had time to ring them up at the Lugano. There was something solidly comforting about the hall porter; Leslie went into the lounge and opened his paper, waiting.

"We must keep calm," Sawley said half an hour later. "Not to make fools of ourselves. There's probably quite a simple explanation but I feel it my bounden duty to ring up the police and ask them if there's been an accident reported last night."

"We must keep calm," he said another half-hour later, "but I have reported her missing. I mean to say, there are such a lot of horrible things happen these days."

"We must keep calm," he said at tea time, "but the police are going to force open the garage doors to see if the car shows any clue as to her whereabouts."

Sawley was not waiting at dinner, he was in the management's office and there were two police cars outside the door, a small black Austin and a large Jaguar.

With the *pêches melbas*, Sawley came into the dining-room. He was wearing his brass-hat uniform which he occasionally wore when he chose the role of commissionaire at the door, but it seemed somehow to have become a little too big for him, or was it that he had become a little too small for it? His face was grey.

There was no need to ask for silence; there was dead silence already.

"We must keep calm," he declared bravely, "but the police would like you all to stay in your places when you have finished dinner. They are coming in to ask you a few questions ... yes, about Miss Lino."

Breathing heavily, he paused for strength to say what he had to say. " Our dear Miss Lino," he reported, " has been found dead on the ground in her garage, beside her car. She has been beaten to death across the head and shoulders," he looked down at the turkey carpet because he was too ashamed at what he had to report to meet anyone's eyes, " and face! " he whispered.

The *pêches melbas* were removed from the dining-room untouched. Nobody wanted any.

PART TWO

Miss Hermione Brown

CHAPTER I

Miss Brown sat rigidly in her chair; she looked like everybody's idea of a cross headmistress, severe face, pursed lips and lowered eyes, to whom some dreadful behaviour on the part of one of her pupils had been reported. Her hands, one on top of the other, were firmly placed in front of her, fingers pressed to the edge of the table and, looking down at them, she had the same impression she used to have when, as a child, she had swung her bare feet in the gently swelling clear seawater, sitting on the breakwater at Port Erin. Her hands looked as though they were waving nebulously like her feet had waved under water: hazy, vague and formless. She had never fainted in her life and she was sure she was not going to do so now; at least . . . nearly sure.

But unfortunately the floor, too, was heaving and waving as though it were a mere sheet under which a strong wind was blowing. She wanted very much to look across at Mr. Dunright but she dare not raise her eyes. Unfortunately, she began to feel worse, blackness was coming from the perimeter of her sight towards the centre so that now she could only see her hands tinily, as though through the wrong end of field glasses. She was beginning to heel over when Mr. Dunright was standing beside her, holding one of her shoulders firmly and preventing her from falling and, with the other hand, pouring out fresh water into her tumbler.

"Here, drink this." She did as she was told.

The other people in the dining-room sat where they were; one old woman was having trouble with her hearing aid and had not heard what Sawley had said; her husband was trying to convey the news to her. No one was hysterical but everyone avoided looking at anyone else and the old trembler had buried his face in his hands.

Feeling better, Miss Brown said so and Mr. Dunright let go of her shoulder, sat down opposite to her and took a draught of water from the same tumbler. He refilled it and drank again.

"I read it in a paper the other day ... 'calamity prone' it said, and I thought that's me all right. 'Calamity prone' and born under Taurus; Lil used to tell me I was lucky when we first married." He went on in a strange way that Miss Brown found terrifying: "I must have done it. I have been acting queer lately. I must have had a black-out and done it!"

"Don't be ridiculous!"

"But folk have black-outs every day. I've been having some queer dreams; I've been acting queer. I haven't hardly known myself these last few weeks since ... since I killed my wife."

"Mr. Dunright, please!" Miss Brown was seriously alarmed. "Please take care of what you are saying." Quite unconsciously she was now wringing those hands over which she had been puzzling. "Take care, take care! The police will be questioning you soon, do take care, I beg you."

Everything she said was hissed across the table almost in a whisper. "The shock is too much for you ... you're unhinged. Do, please, take care; you might get yourself into terrible trouble."

"I am in trouble," he returned bitterly, "who would have done it but me? Who will they suspect but me? With all the toughs and criminal lunatics there are about, they'll never be able to pick out the right one. So they'll pick on me, and maybe I done it, who knows?"

"I know," Miss Brown returned firmly, but she was looking round at their fellow-guests to see if anyone had noticed his remarkable behaviour. "You couldn't, and so that's that."

They stared at each other across the table with the astonishment of two explorers, ill-met by moonlight.

"Didn't you know she was going to be out last night?"
He shook his head.

"She had any number of men friends; there has never been any time when she was without an escort, a male of some kind."

"A male of some kind," he repeated dazedly.

"She is attractive to men . . . she admits it freely."

"Was."

"They'll have to investigate all her male friendships. You and she had just got engaged; what could be more likely than that she told one of her ex-boy-friends and he, in a fit of jealousy, did . . . what he did."

Miss Brown looked round nervously again to see how much they were being observed. "Please listen to me. My father was a solicitor and had quite a lot to do with 'Poor Prisoner's Defence.' When I was a young woman, he often told me about cases which he had to deal with: 'If only,' he used to say, 'if only the suspect would keep his mouth shut. But how they talk; they talk their heads into the noose before anyone has a chance to help them.' That's what he used to say, Mr. Dunright."

"It's fear makes you talk. Fear pulls out the plug, like the plug of the bath, so's the water runs away all in a rush——"

"Sh . . . sh!" She looked round nervously but everybody was too concerned with his or her own reaction to the news to observe the reactions of anybody else.

"Well, you mustn't let it. You've nothing to fear, how could you have? Listen; they might ask you for a statement. Well, on no account give them one." She looked across the table at him. "Will you promise me?"

But he was hardly listening. His face was a sickly yellow and he ran a hand continuously across his forehead.

"Most people, when they think the police have ideas about their guilt, pour out a statement, and always, always, when they have cooled down and have had time to think it over, they regret it. Then they want to make another statement, and that varies from the first. And then, very often, they get things settled in their minds and want to make yet another. So if and when it ever comes to the assizes, or the quarter-sessions or a magistrate's court, it looks terrible. Do you understand?" She paused and said sharply: "Mr. Dunright! Do please listen." She repeated what she had said and Leslie listened, dull-eyed.

"So when it comes to your turn to be questioned, do wait for their questions and answer the simple truth. Don't on any account make a statement; and if they ask you kindly if you'd like to, don't be tempted." She paused: "Will you? Promise me? Please promise!"

It was straightforward.

The sexy youngish woman with plenty of men-friends and ample means; the engagement to a man of her own age with whom she had arranged to go on a holiday.

The motive was not clear-cut but a court of law never spends much time on looking for a motive if there is not an obvious one. Pregnancy and jealousy had almost equal share of importance in the search for motive. There was no question of pregnancy in this case but, quite clearly, jealousy could have motivated the crime.

The old aunt who lunched at Harrods was a rich source of information; she knew her niece had a number of men friends but none of them were what she would call Not Quite Nice. Divorced stock-brokers; ageing bachelor underwriters; the odd French businessman; a brigadier: she could produce their names and some of their addresses and when interviewed by the police, all these were able to supply a satisfactory account of their movements.

The aunt had asked her niece if she had "any new conquests" and, by her rather coy reaction, had gathered that there was a new one, but she had been told nothing further. She was not astonished to hear that it was a man staying in the Hotel Lugano. Her niece liked men; it was the French in her. But she was not immoral, that the aunt could and did swear to. If there were a murderer amongst her niece's friends, it must be the most recent of her men friends, someone she had known only a short time, unless the murder had been done by a passing lunatic, *not* a friend, for gain.

Elizabeth Lyneaux had been found battered to death, lying beside her car in the clothes she had worn for lunch at Harrods. Her handbag, lying underneath the car where it had fallen, contained eighteen pounds in notes, her passport, and a book of traveller's cheques which she had collected from the bank on the day of her death; therefore robbery was not the motive.

She had been hit savagely about the head, shoulders and face by the jack, new and unused since she bought the car, and which was found beside the body. The body was found on the ground at the back of the car, which had been driven straight in. It would seem that Miss Lyneaux had closed the garage doors, or partly closed them, and had opened the tiny boot at the back of her car to put away the starting handle, which, it was thought, she had in her hand. The bag of tools was lying unrolled and, they decided, complete except for the starting handle and the jack which was lying on the ground beside the body and showed blood. It was considered that the doors must have been closed, or almost closed, otherwise the murder would have been seen by people passing along the pavement a few yards directly in front of the garage. One of the doors was bolted top and bottom. The assailant could have done what he did and left her where she was found, dead or dying, between the half door and the back of the car, and gone away quickly, slamming the second half of the door, which would automatically lock itself behind him. The Yale key of the garage door was found in the pocket of the dead woman's linen dress.

The jack of the small car was not of any notable weight; it was considered that anger behind the use of it had made up for the lack of weight in the weapon. Whoever wielded the tool, did so with force which must have arisen from violent anger.

There were no clear fingerprints upon the jack but the plastic bag containing the simple set of tools, was made of a smart simulation of patent leather: it showed several very clear finger, thumb and palm prints.

The last time anyone had seen Miss Lyneaux was when she had gone to her bank in Knightsbridge just before three to get her traveller's cheques and her passport. Her body was found about three o'clock on the following day and during the morning the sun had streamed down on the garage roof, making the heat inside comparable to that of an oven. The time of death, therefore, could not be decided with any degree of accuracy. She had been dead for not less than nineteen hours and not more than twenty-four hours, so there was an uncertainty of about four hours. Nor could it be decided definitely whether she had died at once on being attacked.

The dead woman had been taken by surprise because no screams had been heard. It was suggested that the murder had taken place shortly after three; Miss Lyneaux, her business over, would bring her car back to put it away. It is possible that she was followed either by someone on foot or someone in another car. The assailant had attacked her suddenly and with great violence so that she fell, stunned, by the first blow, possibly backwards against the garage wall; he had then dealt further savage blows as she lay slumped against the wall and, before leaving the garage, he had pulled her forward on to her face so that she could not easily be seen through the window. The whole operation could have taken place in six or seven minutes or less. It could have taken place before a quarter to four because, at that time, the school children of Earl's Court came out of school, where they were collected by their mothers and there would be a number of them about. There were two children in the top flat of the house to which the garage belonged; they usually stayed around playing tig with neighbouring children in the drive and round the side of the house and garage, before their mother called them in to tea. They reported that they had seen and heard nothing and that the garage doors had been closed because they often used their tennis rackets and balls to practice tennis against the closed doors and on that fine May afternoon they had done that for some time.

The evening also being fine, they had gone out after tea and played with the children next door until bedtime, about seven o'clock; during that time they were running about and saw no strange car parked nearby or any strange man near the garage; the doors remained closed.

As a matter of routine, the elderly people in the hotel were questioned. Though some of them had known Miss Lyneaux for years, had lived in the hotel when Miss Lyneaux's father was alive and had been at least as friendly with the old Frenchman as they now were with one another, all of them now evinced complete lack of interest: they knew Miss Lyneaux by sight and that was all. By getting herself murdered, Miss Lyneaux had lifted herself quite out of their order of society. Though they would be willing to help the police in any way they could, it would be quite clear that in this particular case they had no knowledge whatever of any circumstances that might have led to the murder.

Only the shaking old man in Number 5 caused a tremor of interest when he told the police that recently he had heard "sounds" in the night. When asked to specify he refused to do so and simply said darkly that he had ideas as to what they might have been but he wasn't going to say anything. When asked what he meant by "recently" he said: "During the past four or five weeks," which sounded sinister enough since that was the period of Mr. Dunright's stay at the hotel.

The physicist was questioned; he had been working as usual in a laboratory in Euston Road; at five-thirty a friend had called for him in a car and driven him out to a suburban town where he had dined and later given a talk to students at a night class. The friend had driven him back to the hotel, where he had arrived at ten-thirty and gone straight to bed.

Sawley's devotion to duty in the management's absence was notable but it was also clear that his life was at the reception desk at the Lugano; he had a sense of responsibility about the establishment that far transcended that of hall-porter-cum-waiter. It was evident that only Sawley's reliability allowed the management to go away for six months; and, in their absence, the responsibility of the whole running of the hotel lay, finally, on him. There seemed to be no question of his having a weekly day off; Sawley was always there, at his post, keeping a watchful eye on the daily running of the hotel. Late in the evening, after dinner, he would slip out for half an hour to an hour, joining his friends in the public bar of the Double Gloucester and often on a fine afternoon he would stroll to the shops for cigarettes and an early edition of the evening paper. Otherwise he was always around, either in the dining-room, in his tiny basement bedroom, or at the front door and, naturally, Sawley's account of Miss

Lyneaux's movements were those which interested the police most.

Sawley said that he had watched the relationship between Mr. Dunright and Miss Lino " ripening " but that when they told him they were engaged to be married you could have " knocked him down with a feather." However, he had been pleased: Miss Lino would have to settle down sometime and, though he didn't know anything about this Mr. Leslie Dunright, he appeared a nicely-spoken gentleman who gave no trouble whatsoever. It had been all rather sudden, that was all. Mr. Dunright hadn't been there long but then, what did that matter? As far as he knew there was nothing wrong between the two of them; Miss Lino seemed younger than ever, and happy . . . " She was a happy type, always jolly and full of fun, if you know what I mean."

On the day of the murder, Sawley had seen nothing of Mr. Dunright from after breakfast when he had gone off with a business friend, until around midnight. He, Sawley, had been wakened by the sound of a taxi stopping outside and when he went upstairs to see what was happening, he found Mr. Dunright fully dressed and waiting in the lounge; the taxi had been stopping for people going into the next-door house. Mr. Dunright was worried that Miss Lino wasn't home, he could see that at a glance. He'd looked proper poorly. However, he had left him to turn out the lounge light and returned to bed.

Finally, Sawley gave it as his opinion that the police were wasting their time at the Lugano. The murderer was not to be found there but amongst the thugs and thieves of London's underworld. He, personally, didn't attach any importance to the fact that Miss Lino's handbag was found intact; that her pearls and her emerald ring were left on the body. Those two circumstances did not prove that the murderer did not attack her with robbery in mind. He, personally, was quite able to reconstruct the whole affair in theory. Miss Lino had a cheerful jaunty air about her, she might quite well have got into light conversation with a man who, perhaps, asked her the way somewhere; there was no standoffishness about her, far from it; she smiled with equal charm at crossing-sweepers and friends alike. This thug would be hanging around, perhaps offer to shut the garage doors for her and then, once inside the garage, would be seized with the sudden impulse to "do her in." Alone in a small enclosed space with a prosperous-looking woman, he had picked up the first thing that came to hand and bashed her with it; after the primary bash he wouldn't be able to stop and then, when it was all over, he was shocked and sickened by what he had done, had thrown the tool down and run from the spot in horror and terror, slamming the half-door behind him.

Sawley added succinctly: "Men don't like the sight of blood; it turns them sick a lot quicker than it turns a woman. I can see it as clear as clear."

And that is possibly what the police themselves might have thought if it had not been for the extraordinary deportment of Mr. Leslie W. Dunright whose behaviour was such that he might as well have drawn attention to himself in caption as: "murderer third from the left and marked with an X."

That . . . and the palm prints on the tool satchel and Mr. Dunright's inability, or unwillingness, to account satisfactorily for his movements on the day of the murder and to produce anybody with whom he had been on that day and evening.

Personation is a police word for impersonation which, as everybody knows, means to represent in bodily form. If anybody cares to abandon their own identity and take another identity, they are perfectly at liberty to do so; it is not an indictable offence provided that the "cheat," as it is called, is of such a nature that it does not affect the public at large. The law says that "*personation not covered by statute may amount to conspiracy to produce a public mischief by false pretences.*" Thus, it is forgery to make knowingly a false statement upon a passport, or to procure any licence or public money of any kind under a false name.

But in ninety-nine cases out of a hundred, the individual who has changed his identity has not done so for the fun of it, but for some pretty good reason.

Mr. Leslie W. Dunright had appeared at the Hotel Lugano upon a certain date, before which nothing whatever was known about him and in the register he gave the address of a hotel in Paris which did not exist. It did not take the police long to realise that this man was using a false identity but the palm prints did not correspond to any in the files at Scotland Yard, nor did his description tally with that of any wanted or missing man. Their immediate concern was to find the murderer of Miss Lyneaux with the utmost speed and with enough evidence to convict him and get him out of the way. If, in the course of their investigation they discovered that this same man had been involved in one or more other crimes, well and good. If not, not. There being no point in letting him know that they were fully aware of his assumed identity, they kept this assumption to themselves and showed forbearance and understanding when Mr. Leslie Dunright refused to answer any questions that he did not choose to answer.

He made this clear at the outset in a queer little hesitant speech which he had obviously been going over in his mind: " I shall be glad to answer any questions fully that have any bearing on the death of my fiancée Miss Lyneaux because I am as anxious as any of you to discover who killed her. But beyond that my private life is my own."

So it went like this: " How long have you known Miss Lyneaux? "

Answer: " About four weeks."

Question: " In that time you became engaged to her? "

Answer: " Yes."

Question: " You were planning to go on holiday with her? "

Answer: " Yes."

Question: " Can you give us in detail an account of how your palm print comes to be on the tool satchel Miss Lyneaux had in her car? "

Answer: " Certainly. On the morning of her death she asked me to walk to the garage with her to start her car by cranking it with a handle. She was having some battery trouble with a borrowed battery; her own battery was being charged at the service station in readiness for our trip."

Question: " Go on, Mr. Dunright. What happened? "

Answer: " She opened the back of her car and brought the satchel out on to the lowered lid of the boot. I unwrapped it and found the starting handle. As far as I can remember I put the satchel down against the wall and closed the boot whilst she got in to make sure the gear was in neutral. I had to shove the car forward a little from the front; there wasn't a lot of room in front."

Question: " You succeeded in starting up, then? "
Answer: " Oh yes."
Question: " And then what? "
Answer: " She reversed out."
Question: " And what did you do with the starting handle? "
Answer: " For the life of me, Inspector, I cannot be sure but I probably threw it down on top of the satchel against the wall while I closed the garage doors."
Question: " You can't be sure? "
Answer: " How can I be? It was all a perfectly ordinary occasion. I mean, you yourself, if you were asked something like ' Did you put your outdoor shoes on this morning before or after breakfast? ' might have difficulty in answering. If I had known that one of the tools from the bag would be used as a lethal weapon, well, naturally, I would *know* for certain what I did."
Question: " Then you think you tossed it down beside the satchel? "
Answer: " Yes, I think now that I did because later on, when Elizabeth got back, she would see the satchel lying on the floor and would have picked it up, put down the boot lid, and started to pack it away. It was whilst she was doing this that she was attacked, apparently, wasn't it? "
Question: " Whilst she was doing all this, Mr. Dunright, where were you? "
Answer: " I was on business in north-east London."
Question: " With whom? "
Answer: " I can't answer that."
Question: " You say you last saw Miss Lyneaux when she drove away from the garage in the morning. You do not want to tell us where you were all day."
Answer: " Yes. In north-east London."
Question: " What time did you get back to the Lugano? "

Answer: "At about five past eight, I can't be certain."
Question: "Too late for dinner? Weren't you hungry?"
Answer: "On the way home from my business, with a friend, I had some drinks which disagreed with me. I was taken ill and went into the public lavatory in Sloane Square. I spent about ten minutes there and walked back to the Lugano." And then he was very frank about where they had had the drinks and what drinks they were.
Question: "You left your business friend in Sloane Square?"
Answer: "He left me."
Question: "You do understand that this business friend could be of great help to us in confirming this story of yours, don't you, Mr. Dunright?"
No answer.
Question: "Then you prefer not to help either us or yourself in this matter?"
No answer.

CHAPTER II

IT WAS NOT a popular murder; that is, there was nothing unusual about it to fire the public interest. "Woman Found Battered to Death in Earl's Court Garage" had an everyday air about it, a lack of distinction, a rubber-stamp uniformity in the same category as: "Mother of Five Found Strangled in Copse" and "Girl Shot Dead in Local Beauty Spot" and "Stabbed Girl Found in Lovers' Lane."

On the third day the news was reduced to five lines headed "Earl's Court Garage Murder" saying that a man had accompanied the police to the police station in order to assist them in their investigations.

In this case the balance had only just tipped over in favour of an arrest, and it was the suspect's general behaviour more than anything which caused that small extra weight. For instance, when the inspector asked point blank whether he had murdered Miss Lyneaux, the suspect shrugged his shoulders and replied: "If you say so, Inspector." So marked was his apathetic indifference that the inspector told a colleague in confidence that he felt it was his duty to arrest Dunright and let the lawyers and doctors work it out themselves as to whether or not it was a case of diminished responsibility.

The magistrate sent him to the remand prison wearing his second-best suit and his old shoes and told him that he could have visitors at specified times.

The differences of opinion between Miss Brown and Sawley, which had been solely feline, were disregarded in the light of graver issues. Apart from the daily staff and the physicist, who hurriedly vacated his room to stay with a friend during the crisis, these two were the only residents in the hotel under the age of seventy, the only two active people who could now be of assistance to Leslie Dunright. Miss Brown made the approach:

"What do you think, Sawley?"

It was clear that Sawley was deeply affected by the events; he looked tired, ravaged is perhaps the better word. "I'm as certain as God made little apples that he didn't do it, miss."

Miss Brown nodded in agreement.

"But if he did do it, it's not a bad murder," Sawley observed.

"What on earth do you mean?"

"It's a thing that might happen to anybody . . . sudden anger. And once the first blow has been struck they'd have to go on."

"Why?"

"Anger. It works like that, don't it? It dies out quick, they say, a fit of real anger, but not so quick they can stop after the first blow. One blow always leads to another."

"Maybe you're right," she nodded gravely.

"But an arrest isn't the end," Sawley continued. "I believe in justice, British justice above all."

"Do you? The blind goddess?"

"That cuts both ways. She's blindfolded to show she's what-do-you-call-it?"

"Impartial?"

"That's right; couldn't think of the word. Impartial. Mark my words, Miss Brown, if it ever gets as far as the Old Bailey, or I should say when it gets to the Old Bailey, the truth will out."

"But what is the truth?"

"The truth Mr. Dunright didn't do it."

"Then who did?"

"No matter; what the law has to prove is Mr. Dunright did it, and they can't because he didn't."

Miss Brown thought this over. "But Sawley, if one could discover who did it and produce the culprit, as it were, Mr. Dunright would be released automatically and long before it came to trial."

"Too right he would. But so he would if the case collapses."

Miss Brown shook her head this time. "How often does a case collapse? Hardly ever."

"But they do get Not Guilty, quite often."

"I wouldn't be content with that."

"You wouldn't?"

"No, I wouldn't."

The racing page in the folded-across newspaper was in front of him and he was doodling with a pencil round the edges. "But between you and me, Mr. Dunright has always been something of a mystery. You don't get a man of his age absolutely alone in the world without there's somethink fishy. He never got no letters (save one), said they went to his bank. And he had but one friend, as I know of, that Mr. Cross. Now, I ask myself, why don't that Mr. Cross come forward? He says he was with Mr. Cross the day Miss Lino passed on; well, why don't he tell Mr. Cross to come forward to prove it? And the speed with which he got engaged to Miss Lino! Well, miss, I ask you! An adventurer, as they are called in my humble opinion. A ladies' man——"

But Miss Brown could not accept that. "Oh no, Sawley. You're wrong there, I'm sure."

Sawley cocked an eyebrow as he looked at Miss Brown. She went on: "No, not a ladies' man, he was too . . . too, is diffident the word?"

"How do you mean?"

"Too, let's say, uncertain of himself."

After a few minutes thought, Sawley clicked his tongue: "Tck, tck, tck! here we are talking about him in the past already."

"One always does that in hotels," Miss Brown said crossly, "it simply refers to people having left the hotel." She drummed her fingers restlessly on the edge of Sawley's desk.

"Look, miss, would you do me a favour?"

She turned to look at him, with raised eyebrows.

"It's this: go and visit him in the remand prison."

She did not say that was exactly what she had been planning to do.

"I'm sorry for him."

"You are?"

"I think he ... well, it's not for me to say. I don't want to stick out me neck, talk out of turn."

"Go on, Sawley."

"He was under the influence of Miss Lino. She'd got him just there," he pressed his thumb against his folded newspaper. "He didn't know whether he was coming or going. I've known Miss Lino for quite some time now, she was a very ... very ... how shall I put it?"

"Very what?"

"Overpowering, let's call it."

"You thought so?"

Sawley looked uncomfortable. "It isn't exactly that I thought so, as much as you could see he was overpowered. Those green cat's eyes of hers and the way she seemed to make fun of you. You could see he was scared stiff he couldn't ... come up to standard, let's say. First she flattered him to death and then she seemed to mock. Oh, I know I'm talking above my station. It's not for the hall porter to hold forth about those he's supposed to serve. But believe me, Miss Brown, it's those as serves knows all about those they serve."

"So I'm told."

"Yes," Sawley nodded thoughtfully, "I do pride meself

I know a bit about yuman nature; I can't help but. I see all sides of folk doing my job and if I wasn't interested in folk, I'd pack it up."

The dropping of Sawley's aitches was intermittent; for the most part he was careful but, when he became carried away by his own verbosity, they dropped around him like pearls from a broken string. " 'Ere I am, stuck 'ere all day long and what am I stuck 'ere for?"

Miss Brown knew but wanted to hear what Sawley thought, so said she did not know.

"To serve you all," he answered impressively. "I serve, that's my motter, like the Prince of Wales. I serve."

"But then, we all serve, at least, most of us."

"In what way?"

"We serve the community."

"That's not quite the same thing."

"I think it is. I serve people with books."

He thought over the incongruity of the idea and added with a burst of laughter at his own joke: "And doctors serve folk right! But seriously, I'm in service. I'm here at the beck and call of you all. 'Sawley, are there any messages?' 'Sawley, please cancel my Sunday papers!' 'Sawley, please make up the fire!' 'Sawley, somethink is wrong with the television!'

"Sawley this . . . Sawley that. Well, I'm not one to have me face stood on, not by a long chalk. So what? So I study human nature and I sees——"

"What do you see, Sawley?"

"You'd be surprised. One day I'll write me memwars, like that waiter, sorry, head waiter, at that snob restaurant in the West End, only mine'll make much more spicier reading. He only sees them eat . . . I see them eat *and* sleep——"

Miss Brown cleared her throat politely. "I've so enjoyed our little talk," she said. "I shall be going to see Mr. Dunright at Brixton to-morrow afternoon. Is there any particular message you would like to send him?"

"I reckon he could use some fags; I'll get some, miss, and if you'd be good enough to take them and you can tell him from me——" He paused.

Miss Brown, now several paces away from the reception desk, poised for departure, waited.

"You can tell him from me——" but at last words were failing him. He simply made the thumbs-up sign and she turned away, disappointed and wondering if she could reproduce the message adequately.

Miss Brown had been employed at the New Century Library longer than any of her colleagues and it was a matter of mild wonder to some that she had not been made superintendent. Though she had never told anyone, she had been offered the post more than once but each time had refused it: she liked being at the desk W to Z; she liked the borrowers, some of whom she had known for years; she prided herself on knowing exactly what kind of book they would like. She had little bets with herself as to what comment they would make when they brought a certain book back, and sometimes she was right and sometimes wrong.

On the whole, she felt a mild affection for the entire W to Z group which arose, partly, from the undoubted fact that she had a mean little trick of her own by which she was able to keep the latest books, and ones which were very much in demand, back until she had read them herself. This was strictly against the library's rules, and against Miss Brown's principles. But it was her only vice and she indulged it to the full whilst at the same time feeling a rush of affection for those whom she had wronged.

She was not popular with her colleagues, being always very quiet and rarely giving an opinion on any controversial subject. As she never laughed uproariously in the canteen, there were those who said she had no sense of humour. She had a proud little way of walking, with her well-shaped head held high. This was not, in fact, pride, but simply because her glasses were too heavy and would slip down her rather small nose unless she held her head in a certain way. Her glasses were so thick that nobody could see that her eyes behind them were enormous, with that infinitely appealing expression which eyes with very faulty sight can have. Her mouth, too, was full and curly and babyish but nobody ever looked at her mouth, and nobody had ever wanted to kiss it. When people looked at her, they saw only themselves, reflected in miniature in her enormous glasses.

"I say, Brown," somebody shouted at morning coffee, "isn't the Lugano Hotel where you live?"

"Yes."

"Goodness! This murderer, what's-his-name, that bashed the woman in the garage lives there!" The speaker handed Miss Brown the newspaper and pointed to the tiny paragraph at the bottom of page three. She read it and handed it back. Everyone was looking at her.

"Is it true, Brown?"

"Why didn't you tell us?"

"Do you know him?"

"What's he like?"

"He's not a murderer," she snapped. "He's only been arrested."

"Good old Brown."

"Do tell us about it!"

"You *are* a dark horse, old girl!"

"He's not a murderer!" she cried passionately. "He no more murdered her than I did!" She got up from the long trestle table and hurried out. Those who were left exchanged glances, shrugged their shoulders and one said: "She probably did, I wouldn't put it past her!"

She was sizzling when she got back to her desk and summarily dismissed her junior for coffee. And there was old Mrs. Xanopoulos, completely square in a Persian lamb coat: "Oh, I don't like this book at all, dear. So gruesome! Have you got a really nice murder?"

With her elbows propped on her writing-table, Miss Brown held her kitten in her two hands with its latter half hanging down in the inelegant way cats have when suspended and looked at it face to face. For a long time she stared at her kitten and her kitten stared at her with the pupils of its eyes growing larger and smaller and larger and smaller, in perpetual motion, or emotion.

"Well, my ducky, what am I going to do? Something . . .

or nothing? Old spinsters like me are notorious interferers; always minding other people's business. What do you think, darling fluffy little thing?" She put the kitten's face close to her own and kissed it. "So nobody has ever been able to call me a gossip, or an interfering old cat (sorry dear), or a busybody. So far." She paused again. "But now, my little cockney alley-kitten, I seem to be the only person in the whole wide world who knows that Mr. Leslie Dunright is Mr. Leslie Williams, Rockhaven Mansions, Ealing, W. Is that a good thing, or a bad thing?"

Putting the kitten down on a rug which lay folded on her bed for the purpose, Miss Brown brought out an old battered cash box, unlocked it carefully and took from it a clean but crumpled handkerchief, containing fragments of burnt paper, the charred stub of a cheque book and a few brown curled pages from a backless passport.

Something more than chance, Miss Brown thought: Fate herself had left in the passport the profession, date and place of birth and description of the holder on page two and the photograph on the opposite page. The back had been torn off and the main fabric had been torn hurriedly in half, the bottom half having been more extensively burnt whilst the top half had almost escaped. The name Williams appeared quite legibly through the light brown scorching of the top half and Leslie emerged even more clearly from the bottom half.

She already knew the details by heart but once again she went over them to make sure that she had them correctly.

As the daughter of a solicitor and a prolific reader of every kind of book, Miss Brown's mind had been conditioned to such a contingency as the present one and, though entirely inexperienced, her reasoning was not without pith.

Thinking over her recent discussion with the redoubtable Sawley, one large fallacy filled her mind. In Sawley's opinion, the law had to prove that Mr. Dunright was the murderer but what Miss Brown had learned was that the onus was upon the defence to prove him innocent; the difference was subtle.

The grave and disturbing feature was that he had already been arrested and remanded in custody and, in the minds of

three-quarters of those who were interested, he was already
"the garage murderer." The police were far too busy and
understaffed to spend any more time digging up data about a
man for whom they already had enough evidence for an
arrest.

As far as Miss Hermione Brown could see, there was
nobody, absolutely not a single soul anywhere, who was going
to do anything more for Mr. Leslie Dunright. And clearly,
Mr. Leslie Dunright was not going to do anything more for
himself. The Justices would have granted him a certificate for
free legal assistance, there being some doubt as to his means,
and the defence solicitor would be presented with the facts, as
they now appeared, which, in turn would be put before the
counsel he employed. There would be a great many words
written and spoken before the case was over, but nobody was
going to take the trouble to find out anything more about
the accused.

There was, therefore, no question of her being a busy-
body; as she now saw it, it was her absolute duty to do what
she could for Mr. Dunright and providence had already
firmly pointed the way by insisting that she pick up from the
hearth the charred remains of whatever it was that Mr.
Dunright had been burning that first evening he came to the
Lugano.

A serious aspect of the case was time. Tied to her desk at
the library for eight hours of every weekday, and every other
Saturday morning, she had little time to spare. It might be
some while before the trial at the Central Criminal Court, or
it might be three weeks ahead, which would give her only four
and a half days for the digging-out of fresh evidence which
would be acceptable at Law and which she knew existed.

Miss Brown wrapped up the fragments and carefully
stowed away her treasure box. Then she slid up the window,
delighting in the ease with which it could be raised since the
fitting of the new left-hand sash cord, stepped out on to the
leads, leaned over the parapet and set her kitten's dangling
feet safely upon the six-inch ledge which ran along the whole
length of the terrace between the ground and first floors.
From here the clever kitten, by devious paths, along, round and

down the vagaries of the early Victorian architecture, achieved solid earth in the savoury region of the dustbins. Miss Brown smilingly watched it out of sight then returned to her room and prepared her plan of campaign.

CHAPTER III

THERE WAS a look of grievous anxiety upon his face when he was escorted into the visiting-room and it was replaced instantly by an expression of disappointment so great that Miss Brown was shocked into saying: " I'm not the visitor you expected! I'm sorry! " He flopped on to the hard chair as though his legs had given way.

" Miss Brown! " He brought out his pocket handkerchief and wiped it quickly across his forehead. " How kind of you to come."

A little deflated, she took from her brown leather bucket bag the things she had brought him: the hundred cigarettes from Sawley, the box of dates and the two packs of cards from her.

" I know you don't read much but you might play patience."

He smiled a little: " I used to. I played Racing Demon with my mother, and bezique."

" There you are, then. A good way of passing the time."

She asked him about the conditions under which he was living and the companions he was with and then conversation flagged a little. He looked completely deflated. She decided not to waste any more time and came directly to the heart of the matter. She wanted to help him, she said, and if he would tell her in what way she could help him best, it would make things much easier for them both. They talked about money; as she had thought, he had been granted legal aid and the solicitor was bringing counsel to see him in a day or so. With regard to his " cash in hand " as he called it, that had been put in the office safe and was doled out to him as he required it. She longed to ask him if that was all he had but felt she could not do so until their friendship had advanced a bit farther.

With some twiddling of the handle of her bag and the avoidance of looking straight at him she managed to get out: " Mr. Dunright, I feel you are so very much alone in this." She leaned forward impulsively and put her gloved hand on his. " You remember what you said at the time of shock, when you heard Elizabeth had been killed? " She paused but pressed on: " Do you remember? "

For a moment he avoided the point in question.

" I remember what *you* said and very useful it has been. I took the advice you gave me. Thanks."

" I mean, what you said about your wife. Lil you called her," she persisted.

" It was the shock," he mumbled.

" I know. But wouldn't it be a good thing to tell me now? "

He shook his head. " There's nothing needs knowing. Nothing in the past that would help me now."

" Are you sure? "

" Certain. It's the only certain thing left. There is a past, I'll admit. I walked out of that with, shall we put it, with dirty hands? But that's all. I didn't kill my wife nor anything like it. I got the biggest shock in the world when I found her dead, and turning it over and over in my mind, it's grown on me to such an extent I blurted out that . . . that rubbish." He gave her a quick furtive look. " Do you believe me? "

" I don't know why I should, but I do."

He looked so crushed that she went on: " Well, I do know why I should." She glanced at the clock, at the nearby group of visitors talking to another prisoner, at the indifferent warders. "There's not much time so we must talk about essentials, mustn't we? I believe you because you have the one quality I look for in a man. You're kind. It doesn't follow at all that because you're kind you're truthful but because I know you're kind I know you didn't murder Elizabeth. You couldn't. You couldn't hit a soft, living thing with a hard piece of iron; it would hurt you as much as it hurt them, as they say. And you couldn't have killed your first wife for the same reason."

" That was an overdose of barbiturates."

" The same idea. You couldn't make anybody ill. You're

kind, you see?" As though she had proved some great truth she sat back, looking satisfied. The warders had begun to be restive; one of them was rocking backwards and forwards from his toes to his heels and staring up at the ceiling as though counting the passing seconds.

He leaned forward: "Look, I understand you're being wonderful to me and I do want you to realise I'm not 'withholding information,' as the police have called it. I'm absolutely certain that anything in my past isn't going to help me now. It's quite the reverse. If I were to tell you anything more it would put a burden on you which you needn't have. It would be saddling you with an unnecessary weight and to no purpose whatever."

"What about this man who has called several times at the Lugano?"

His face looked blank as though he was about to deny any such visitor.

"I mean the spivvy-looking person, flashily dressed, with that great pale blue American car. Don't forget that I have a private box, right above the front door. I can see everything that goes on from there, and a great deal I don't want to see, believe me. I could hardly miss that visitor and that car! I have watched you arriving home on several evenings."

He drew in a deep breath, his nostrils widening. "Ah, there you have it. If he came forward he might put me in the clear."

"Could he?"

"He certainly could. I was working for him all that afternoon selling goods for him in a market in north-east London. That particular evening, after the time they reckon Elizabeth was killed, I was having drinks with him in the Strand. I left him in Sloane Square and round about seven-thirty started to walk back to the hotel."

Miss Brown could barely contain her excitement. Her voice rose to a squeak but she instantly controlled it on receiving a disapproving look from the warder. "Have you told the police that?"

"I haven't given them details."

"But why not?" she asked in an agony of impatience.

He drew in a deep breath again. "Because he has me there."

"You mean . . . he's not an honest man and could blackmail you?"

"Miss Brown, aren't you surprised to hear that I've been selling in an open market?"

"Nothing ever surprises me, Mr. Dunright."

"Well, I've surprised myself. I'm a bank cashier, not an itinerant salesman. There are reasons why I can't tell the police what I was doing, in detail. I said I was at a movie."

Miss Brown was almost hugging herself with exasperation. "Please, please tell me more," she hissed, with a wary eye on the warder.

"There should be nothing on this earth to stop this chap coming forward and saying I was with him."

"Why doesn't he, then?"

"Because, as I must have known all along, though I've never admitted it to myself, the things he got me to sell were either stolen, or smuggled or come by in some dishonest way. He had a lot to say about it all being above-board. But I know now . . . oh, I've got plenty of common sense *now*." He gave an audible sneer at himself. "I had then, but I wanted the cash more than I wanted to think."

"Oh dear! You are in a mess."

He made no reply; the absurd understatement floated into the stuffy air and it was time to go.

"Quick," she brought out a pencil and her diary, "tell me the name of the market . . . and the man . . . and what you sold——"

"Come along now," the warder said kindly, but she had time to scribble down the monosyllabic answers.

He was standing up now and, almost as an afterthought, he said: "Please don't tire yourself on my behalf. I'm not worth it, honestly. You'll never trace Charlie Cross. That may not even have been his name."

"If you're going around doing things against the law and under an assumed name, you shouldn't do it in a car like that," she stated, popping her diary back into her handbag.

"I'm past praying for," he said drearily. "It may be that

it would do me good to have a ten-year stretch in prison. What I need."

"Don't talk such absolute nonsense. Besides, it would be a miscarriage of justice. A life-sentence isn't automatically reduced to ten years; you've got to work for it. And have you thought of this: they might even turn this into a capital murder, if they could prove theft. And you know the penalty for that!"

This was hardly the thing to say when visiting someone remanded for murder but it had the effect of wiping the apathetic expression from his face and bringing a sharpness back into his eyes.

"So, please," she ended, "please think up anything you can to help yourself and I'm going to help you all I can. So don't worry . . . too much!"

If anything were needed to endear him to Miss Brown he said it now, with the warder standing patiently by the door, holding it open.

"There's no sense in it," he said sadly. "Elizabeth has known a lot of men in her time but why didn't any of them marry her? Then I come along. I haven't known her long, Miss Brown, but I loved her and wanted to look after her. And what happens? She's battered to death and the one person who really loves her and wouldn't hurt a hair of her head . . . he's the one who's supposed to have done it. It doesn't make sense. Good-bye, and thank you for coming." And then, once more, with hands outspread, he said: "It doesn't make sense!"

CHAPTER IV

Miss Brown stepped off the trolley bus with about thirty-five other people and looked nervously about her. The wilds of outer north-east London were unexplored territory to her and she felt out of her element. There was no need to ask where the market was; she went with the stream, clutching her handbag, which she had made doubly secure by pulling the handle over her arm and keeping the wide-open top of her bucket bag firmly closed with her other hand. It was a fine afternoon with a fresh breeze blowing in from the North Sea. This delightful sea-breeze was marred by the smell of frying which came in occasional vaporous patches, the smell of the jellied eel and winkle stall, the smell of the second-hand clothes stalls, and the smell of the caged birds stall.

There was a holiday feeling about; gone were the anxious housewives counting every halfpenny; money was being unwisely spent, thrown about, in fact. There was a light-hearted atmosphere; those who had never had any money to spare, who had led drab and colourless lives, were now buying the gay and colourful things which appealed to them: brightly coloured artificial flowers; budgerigars; candy floss; bikinis; sports shirts in rock'n'roll colours; costume jewellery. Miss Brown was a little taken aback and bewildered. She had planned to ask every other stall holder where Mr. Charlie Cross had his pitch, starting at the first one she came to and working her way round the whole market. It was at once obvious that this was going to be a much more difficult task than she had visualised. However, she bravely set to work. The stall holders were so busy selling that often she had to start her question several times before receiving attention. Once or twice she was brushed off as though she were a fly. But in the main she was given a fragment of their attention: " What, dear? Never 'eard of 'im! "

One man was selling identical plastic bags in a variety of

colours. His wife was behind him pulling more and more stock out of a packing case. "What say?"

"Mr. Charlie Cross."

"What's he deal in?"

"A variety of things, I believe," Miss Brown murmured.

"All sorts, eh? No, I don't know yer Charlie Allsorts, dear. Go and ask the market superintendent, he'll know."

"Oh, thank you!" Miss Brown returned gratefully.

The market superintendent was wearing a brown pin-striped suit with a metal plate as big as a saucer proclaiming his officialdom, hanging from his lapel, almost obliterating him, and a peaked uniform cap worn on the back of his head. He was chewing a piece of straw and seemed to be good-humoured enough. "Charlie Cross, m'dear? Never 'eard of him. What's he sell?"

"All sorts of things," Miss Brown said helpfully.

"Oh, one of those." He whistled through his doubtful teeth. "Are you sure you got the name right?"

"No, I'm afraid not."

He shrugged. "Well, there you are! I wish I could 'elp, but you've giv' me nothink to go on."

Miss Brown was about to say with injured dignity that she had no reason to suppose she had not got the name right when she realised that she had no reason to suppose that she had. What a hopeless thing it was, looking for somebody who may have a false name, who employed someone else who did have a false name, to sell a variety of unspecified and nameless *things*.

She thanked the superintendent politely. Lack of success was very tiring; one small hopeful event would have put new energy into her. She stood at a refreshment stall and had a cup of very nasty tea and a moribund sausage roll which made her feel a great deal worse. When she reached the States' china and glass stall she was showing distinct signs of wear; one or two fronds of shiny hair had escaped from the immaculate pile; her face was paler than usual and her whole figure sagging from the shoulders. But it didn't matter how busy she was, Mrs. State always had time for other people. Miss Brown approached her confidentially and Mrs. State misunderstood: "Over there, dear, on the right, just by the car park, see?" she pointed.

Miss Brown shook her head. "It's not that. Mr. Charlie Cross. Do you know him?"

Mrs. State stroked one of her chins thoughtfully: "Do you mean Charlie, by any chance?"

Miss Brown nodded enthusiastically. "Probably."

"Oh, Charlie!" Mrs. State was delighted that they had a mutual acquaintance. "But he's not bin near for, ooh, days."

Mr. State, ever vigilant and jealous, was casting suspicious glances at Miss Brown. "Lady's asking for Charlie," his wife explained.

Mr. State jerked his thumb over his shoulder, which might have meant anything. Mrs. State said: "We reckon his friend Perce must of died."

"Perce———?" Miss Brown was bewildered.

"His friend."

"That was Mr. Dunright!"

"Dunright? You mean the gentleman sold for him two-three times? No, that's not Perce. Charlie and Perce 'as bin together years. Then Perce was took ill and was hospitalised, ooh, some weeks past now."

Miss Brown's head was beginning to ache rather badly, in spite of the pleasant sea breeze.

Mrs. State pointed again: "His pitch was over there, see, where that space is. He's not been there not for quite some time, as I say."

"You wouldn't know where he lives? Where I could get hold of him?"

"No idea, sorry. They come and they go, you know, they come and they go!"

"Come on, Bessie!" Mr. State shouted in a voice like a fog horn.

"So long, dearie, sorry I can't help!"

And Miss Brown walked away without learning that Mrs. State had been the source from which she had achieved her new kitten. She was now so tired that she could not bring herself to ask another stall holder for Charlie Cross. It was much easier to walk up and down the lines of parked vans, pick-ups, trucks, convertibles and saloon cars, looking for the pale blue Chevrolet. She knew it would not be there but to search the car park had been part of the plan and she must follow it doggedly, so that she would not have to come back in the future to carry out something she had omitted to do.

She walked determinedly up and down the lines and when, finally, she found herself examining the scooters, mopeds and bicycles all parked together at the end, she knew it was time to go home.

At dinner time Sawley leaned over her as he served the soup.

"How was he?" He put his head closer to hear Miss Brown's reply and she found herself staring into the wilderness of his hairy ear. Furthermore, so great was his anxiety that his thumb was partially immersed in the brown windsor soup, a solecism for which she had often heard him berating his underling in excoriating prose.

"Not good!" she returned shortly.

With the fish he hissed: "Pleased with the fags?"

"Oh, yes!"

With the overdone beef and the dab of horseradish sauce, he said something which Miss Brown did not quite catch about Mr. Dunright's nerves playing him up. And with the ubiquitous *pêche melba* he said that it was a long lane that had no turning, was what he always said.

But Miss Brown could not forget the expression on Mr. Dunright's face when he had said: "I loved her and wanted to look after her!" It had haunted her on the long journey out to the market, on her fruitless search of the market place, and on the long way home. She could still see it.

Avoiding coffee in the lounge, she went straight upstairs to her room, took off her laced-up shoes, and, picking up her kitten from the rug where it was curled smugly, she tucked it under her chin and lay down on the bed, gently scratching the top of its head.

CHAPTER V

ALL THE LONG night, during which Miss Brown had slept fitfully, waking with a start and having what she called "cat naps," Rockhaven Mansions, Ealing, shone in her mind like the morning star. She understood perfectly that Mr. Dunright was convinced that nothing about his past, himself as Leslie Williams, could be any help in his present situation. Nevertheless, if she was going to be of any further help to him in his fearful predicament she must find out something about this other life of his in order that she might make her own assessment and either proceed or not proceed, as the circumstances would dictate. So far, in her life, she had adhered rigidly to the principle of not prying into other people's affairs but now this same principle seemed shoddy. She must press on in the crusading spirit and, if what she discovered were to shock and horrify her, what did it matter?

After breakfast it was raining with the rather pleasant gentle rain of early summer, so she put on her drizzle boots, her green plastic mackintosh, tied a triangle of green plastic material round her hair, fed her kitten with fluid made from powdered milk and half a sardine, put it out on the leads, closed the window and hurried downstairs, past the dining-room where Sawley and his minion were clearing away the last of the late breakfasts, and hurried out without a word to him.

The kitten had become very adept at the journey down from the first floor. It was now pushing its way along the inside of the railings round the area, and, when it saw her, leered through the railings at her. But Miss Brown had her umbrella up and did not even see it as she hurried along the wet, empty Sunday street.

Rockhaven Mansions was only a short walk from Ealing tube station, a fairly modern pre-war block of flats situated back from the road and giving the impression of being unfinished, like pieces of bookcase bought section by section. There was an appreciable patch of worn-out grass between the road and the flats, and a gravel drive, now crowded with garage-less cars.

Miss Brown walked hurriedly past and past again. The third time she walked quite slowly. The rain had almost cleared and one or two children were rushing about. It was not the class of flat with an attendant porter but she hoped there would be some kind of resident janitor and with this idea in mind, she walked round the back where a number of coke piles showed that she was not far from the boilerhouse and stoke-hole. There was, in fact, a gangling youth shuffling about in dungarees whom she at once approached.

But maybe this was not Miss Brown's lucky day any more than yesterday had been. The youth had a hare lip and a cleft palate and it was completely impossible to make out more than one of twelve words he splashed out hollowly.

Thanking him politely, she went round to the front and deliberately and slowly walked past the entrances. There were half a dozen of these under doorless arches, each leading to six flats and the names of the flat-dwellers were conveniently displayed in white painted letters on a board inside. Against the indicator of Flat No. 2, in the fifth entrance, was the name *Mr. and Mrs. Leslie Williams.*

Miss Brown's heart gave a jerk which set her pulse racing and, turning away in shock, she found herself a few feet from the dirty pale blue Chevrolet, parked in the drive immediately opposite the opening.

And now thought was entirely suspended; she was a thing of throbbing emotion, she simply stood still and vibrated, awaiting happenings.

Almost at once an apparition came round the corner into the drive pushing a flat barrow of Sunday newspapers. He was wearing tight trousers and a black velvet lumber jacket. Round his neck was a gold chain with a large crucifix which tapped regularly against the zip of his jacket as he walked. He wore a big pewter ring on his middle finger and had long hair with side pieces the size of small bedside mats. He greeted Miss Brown with a handsome smile which encouraged her to ask him at once if he was going up to Mr. and Mrs. Williams's flat.

"Na-ow," he returned and explained that he simply shouted like this (and he gave a wild cry like an orang-outang calling to its mate), and they came and got it.

They did indeed. Almost before Miss Brown had time to step back, he was surrounded by the residents buying two and more papers. When, apparently, the right number of people had been served, the barrow-boy tidied up his papers and prepared to leave but his attention was taken by a cry from above and, looking up, Miss Brown saw, leaning from the window and shouting instructions to "hold it a sec," the face for which she had been searching.

Mr. Charlie Cross was *en déshabille* and, when he arrived a minute later to buy his papers, it was clear that he had thrown on a shirt and literally jumped into a pair of trousers which he had not even had time to adjust properly. With his powerful neck emerging from his open-collared silk shirt, he was a handsome sight indeed, like Clark Gable in *Mutiny on the Bounty* Miss Brown decided, tender-eyed.

She darted across to entrance number five and stood directly in his path as he returned from the barrow, a cigarette hanging from his lips, his eyes scanning the front page photograph of the intrepid Serpentine bather in a bikini.

She said: "Mr. Cross," but she was breathless from shock and her voice came out barely audible. She tried again: "Mr. Cross!"

He looked up: "Um?"

"You are Mr. Charlie Cross, aren't you?"

"Correct."

"Aren't you a friend of Mr. Leslie Dunright?"

Charlie took the mauled cigarette from his mouth, wrenching it from where it had stuck to his lower lip. He stared at it as though astonished to find it there. "No," he said at last.

"Oh, Mr. Cross, you are! I know you quite well by sight!"

"Oom 'ave I the pleasure of addressing?"

"I——" she brought out a pocket handkerchief and dabbed her mouth to give herself time to decide whether or not she should say who she was. He was waiting and looking ominous rather than angry. " I, too, am a friend of Mr. Dunright."

" So? "

" So I have come to ask if you will help him."

Charlie turned on the charm with which he was richly endowed. " My dear lady," his voice was full of concern, " I should so like to help you but I don't know a ruddy thing about your friend Mr. Dunright! "

" Mr. Williams, then," she said, desperately, passionately, unwisely.

And now Charlie was still and tense. He held the cigarette between his nicotine-stained finger and thumb and the smoke rose in a straight blue line between them as he stared at her.

" So," he said at last, " a policewoman. I see."

She neither admitted nor denied it but pressed on, appealing to what she knew everybody possessed—his decent feelings. " He has been arrested for murder, as I am sure you know. And you are the only person who can clear him."

" Me? " he seemed about to deny everything but changed his mind. " I'm not having nothink to do with this job, you can take that straight. He's bound to get himself into trouble, that one; there's nothink I can do or say."

Miss Brown shook her umbrella in anger but decided it best to appear merely to be shaking the rain drops off.

" You know that's not so, Mr. Cross."

And now he was turning nasty, the charm was gone and he pushed his face close to hers and snarled: " You don't know a darn thing, not a darn thing. What would you say if you knew your Mr. Williams was wanted for embezzlement . . . and wife murder? "

" I wouldn't believe a word of it," Miss Brown returned at her firmest, " not a word. You're trying to frighten me." And he had succeeded.

" I can't stand here any longer." He started up the pseudo-marble stairs. " I'd run off home and sleep on it if I was you."

He was moving away rapidly and Miss Brown was forced

to shout her Parthian shot, like an angry gipsy whose white heather has been rejected, shouting curses altogether out of proportion to the offence: "It's all very well but I've got you in the end. The Crown Office will serve you with a subpœna, do you hear, Mr. Cross?"

There was silence but she could see the fingers of his stubby hand over the edge of the balustrade. He was pausing to listen and she went on: "And if you don't know what a subpœna is, you soon will! It means you'll be forced to go to court and give evidence——"

And then the door of one of the ground floor flats opened and a woman whose head was covered with sausage-shaped curlers looked out and asked if anything was wrong.

It was all too humiliating and vile and strongly reminiscent of an ugly scene cutting into her early youth when her parents had dismissed a dishonest maid who stood on the doorstep for hours shouting curses until the police had to be sent for to remove her.

As Miss Brown hurried away, tears of chagrin were streaming down her face so profusely that her glasses were almost opaque and she weaved from side to side like a drunkard.

Round the corner and a few steps along was one of those tiny establishments peculiar to London and usually identifiable by the presence of driverless taxicabs outside. They are being gradually smartened up with modern décor and a whining espresso coffee machine but the original type is still to be found. They have a counter immediately inside the door, with a small aisle between it and a single line of tables, often with a long bench against the opposite wall. It is not easy to see the attendant for the enormous show case on the counter, containing a variety of eatables, and an equally vast urn outfit and the whole is punctuated by numerous coloured cards advertising soft drinks.

Only very exceptional circumstances would have driven Miss Brown into one of these "caffs"; these were that it was Sunday morning in the suburbs, with no hope of finding a tea room open, and that she was shaking violently so that her legs would not carry her any farther. She went inside and flopped down on the first chair she saw. There were no other customers, it had been opened only a few minutes; the proprietor, a mean-looking, cross man, was not quite ready for customers. She asked for a pot of tea and, whilst he prepared it, she untied the plastic triangle and took off her plastic drizzle boots. She would have liked to go to the ladies' room but, after a quick look round, decided against asking to be directed to it, tidying her face and hair as best she could with the aid of her compact mirror.

The tea was much too strong but had considerable reviving powers; with the third cup she began to try to sort things out. She was by nature peace-loving; she did not enjoy a scrap and it seemed that she had now, in the space of a few minutes, got herself a full-blown enemy. That was what came, she told herself, of sticking her neck out. But what else could she do? Very few people, when it came to the point, walked unconcernedly along the river bank when the drowning man was shouting for help. However much they might deplore interference, they did interfere when it came to a matter of life and death.

It was perfectly clear that, if Charlie Cross had been a friend of Leslie Dunright before the shocking death of Elizabeth Lyneaux, he was no longer a friend now. For reasons of his own, he intended to keep out of it. And not so much from choice, she guessed shrewdly, as from necessity.

Was it possible that the fragments of burnt passport she had found belonging to Leslie Williams had been stolen from Leslie Williams, whoever he might be, by Leslie W. Dunright and that she had been utterly wrong in thinking that Leslie Williams had been trying to destroy evidence of a previous identity? A hot wave of colour flooded her face as she remembered the ridiculously sentimental gesture she had made in sending Leslie Dunright a birthday card on the birthday of Leslie Williams, as it appeared on the passport.

How had it been possible to make such a fool of herself? She was now obliged to analyse her absurd gesture and found the result revolting.

Could it be that Charlie Cross was Leslie Williams? And who was Charlie Cross's friend Perce to whom Mrs. State of the market had referred? And why was Charlie Cross living in Ealing in a flat under the name of Leslie Williams? Or, alternatively, why was Charlie Cross calling himself Leslie Williams or vice versa? Was it because Charlie Cross was living in Ealing as Leslie Williams that he would not, could not, come forward to the police to clear Leslie Dunright? Was the thing he was hiding so serious that he could let Leslie Dunright be convicted of a murder he had not committed rather than come forward?

Miss Brown drank the now nearly cold tea. If it were so serious, then Charlie Cross would now be making preparations to see that she could not carry out her threat to cause him to be served with a subpoena. He would be leaving Rockhaven Mansions at the earliest possible moment, and, almost certainly, taking his ridiculous car with him. And if he had any sense, she thought in parenthesis, he would dispose of the monstrous car in favour of something a little less noticeable.

Hermione Brown now felt slightly dizzy and unreal because she knew she was about to do something which, on the surface, sounded wildly improbable but which, as she saw it, was the only thing she could do. She was going back to Rockhaven Mansions to sit in the car until such time as he came out. No, she was not going to slip down inside and hide, she was going to occupy the front seat, beside the driving wheel, and simply sit, imperturbable and importunate, until he got into the car beside her. After which she would stay where she was until she knew something more about the whole affair. If the car were locked, then she would stand beside it.

And this would be brave but not as brave as it sounded, because nothing very much could happen to her in full view of the flat-dwellers. And if Mr. Cross were to drive off with her he would hardly dare to dispose of her violently when there would be dozens of witnesses to the undoubted fact that he had driven off with her.

She had done certain things a great deal braver in the air raids, years ago, the difference, however, being that those brave deeds had been done in the heat of the moment whereas this was being done in the coldest of cold lights of reason.

The café was less than a minute's walk from Rockhaven

Mansions; she looked hopefully at the busy proprietor. How much easier it would make it if she were to ask him casually if he knew a Mr. Charlie Cross and he were to come over with a concise account of the man, telling her all she could possibly want to know about him as he impinged on the business in hand, which was what would happen in one of the books she was in the habit of reading. Things didn't happen that way in real life . . . you had to do your finding out the hard way. She sighed heavily. The concentrated stare she was giving the man, combined with the sigh, were liable to misconstruction and had just that effect. He ceased to look preoccupied and cross and, leaning across the counter familiarly, he gave her a really nasty leer. " Anythink else you'd like ? "

" A packet of biscuits, please, and . . . er . . . one of those Mars bars." As he wrapped them in a bag he remarked: " A stranger in these parts ? "

She nodded. " Do you happen to know any of the people living in that block of flats round the corner ? "

" Rockhaven Mansions ? Bless you, yes. They're not regular customers, not my class of customer, I should say, but they do come in for fags, and sandwiches to take home. Oh yes, Rockhaven Mansions, very nice too."

She slipped the paper bag of provisions into her handbag: " Would you know anyone called Cross ? "

He shook his head.

" Or Williams ? "

Once more he could not help, and waited with an air of slightly lecherous expectancy.

She picked up her mackintosh from where it hung over the back of the chair she had been using, put the plastic triangle in the pocket, folded it and handed mackintosh, umbrella and drizzle boots over the counter.

" I wonder if you would be good enough to look after these for me ? Brown is my name, Hermione Brown and I live at the Lugano Hotel, South Kensington. I will come back for my things."

" I'll put them down here, under the counter, see ? That's okay."

She paid for the tea and the purchases and, as she left, she turned back and said wistfully: " You won't forget the name, will you? "

" Brown."

" Hermione Brown."

It was almost as though she were saying good-bye to herself.

CHAPTER VI

THE BLUE CAR was still there; furthermore it was unlocked. With her head held very high, her back very straight and the lobes of her ears tingling, she stepped inside, sat down in the passenger's seat in front and pulled the door to with an expensive clunk. The children, playing in the now fitful sunshine, gave her a casual look and went on with their game, which seemed to be a kind of new-style grandmother's footsteps with much shouting and banging of toy pistols. People came and went with Sunday-morning leisure; cars and an occasional taxi arrived and left but no one approached the blue car. Towards one o'clock, the children were called in and activity slowed down till it almost ceased.

The tension had slackened, she began to feel more relaxed but was nagged by the thought that what she was doing was, in her mother's words, " importunate," an adjective that no well-brought-up female allowed to be applied to herself.

She pulled off her gloves and looked at her hands, two friends with whom she had a life-long familiarity. She was surprised to find them there with her on this adventure, looking exactly as they always looked; quite ordinary little hands but now attached to someone unfamiliar and alien. She sympathised with them, feeling on the side of her bewildered hands.

She thought of Leslie Dunright, his bright pink and white boyish complexion, his thin brown hair, already receding in great gulfs on either side of his forehead; the nervous way he had of running his tongue across his lips, like a school-boy asked to admit to a lie; the confused expression in his eyes.

Why was she doing this? She had read her Freud, her

Adler and her Jung. Freud would put it all down to sex, and nothing but sex. Jung would say it was regression to infantility, and Adler would say it was a transference of the libido as the result of unconscious inferiority. Everybody else would say it was because she was a repressed spinster. Everybody, in fact, thought all spinsters frustrated because they were spinsters; a typical male concept, she thought wryly.

But because she had an open mind and gave every idea her due consideration, Hermione Brown now faced the question. Was she " in love " with Leslie Dunright? Would she like him to make love to her? She thought this over carefully and decided that she would not. Did she, then, feel towards him, the unfulfilled mother-love that she might have? She thought this over, too. Nobody was less of a mother than she; children got on her nerves, she did not understand them. So it could hardly be that.

Nor was it excessive gratefulness for his small kindnesses; finding a new kitten for her; mending the sash cord. No, that reason was inadequate.

What was it, then? Looking down at her quiet folded hands, Miss Brown was forced to admit that she did not know.

Nor could she know that heredity was the most likely reason. A great-aunt on the distaff side had believed so passionately in justice for women that she had chained herself to a tree in the Mall and had subsequently spent a month in Holloway Gaol for causing the nose of a Metropolitan policeman to bleed profusely during a scuffle in Trafalgar Square.

Behind the militant aunt was a long thin line of Englishmen through which ran a vibrant belief in the maintenance of Right; here and there, along this line, some had fallen by the wayside, suffering awful mutilation in the cause of Justice.

And now this daughter of time sat in her strategic position and ate her cheese sandwich and her Mars bar to keep up her strength to battle for this same threadbare but still unextinguished principle.

Introspection had a mildly soporific effect; that and the fact that nothing happened caused her to feel relaxed and then sleepy. It was time for the Sunday afternoon siesta; the children having been firmly anchored to the TV, the parents were having a nap. On one window-sill she could see a tortoiseshell cat curled up in the sun. She hoped her own little cat would be doing the same thing in South Kensington on her private balcony. It was warm in the car now; she sighed, thinking of the cat before this one. She had never had a cat cut off in its prime. All her cats lived happy and peaceful lives and died in their own beds, mourned over by her. But this cat . . . she would always feel sorry about it, it was such a poor little thing with one ragged ear that would never stand up, and the eyes that were of different colours. She knew a cat with this distinction brought good luck and, when it disappeared, the even tenor of life at the Lugano was disturbed; yes, it dated from then. The day it vanished, Leslie Dunright had appeared. And since then nothing had been quite the same, culminating in the awful disaster to poor Elizabeth.

Come to think about it, Elizabeth had started showing-off the very first evening he had appeared. There hadn't been an apparently single man at the hotel for months, or even years, and Elizabeth had made what Miss Brown called " a dead set " at him. It had made her ashamed of her sex to be compelled to observe the way in which Elizabeth had thrown herself at him, clearly a little man who knew nothing much about women.

She " played with fire," Miss Brown told herself, compressing her lips, and women who did that quite often got themselves murdered. Too free with men by a long way. How was one ever to know, ever to find out, how she had met her end so disgracefully? Luncheon at Harrods with the aunt . . . but what afterwards? Elizabeth had thought nothing of going into a pub and having drinks all by herself. And at any licensed hour of the day! She could perfectly visualise Elizabeth seeing her aunt off home after that luncheon, saying she was on her way to the bank, and, once the aunt had disappeared: " Phew, for a drink! " and going into the next expensive-looking bar she came across.

Any jazzy-looking bar in London. How could anybody who might have seen her sipping her dry Martini and having one of her ridiculously frivolous flirtations with any stray man, already well on the way to being drunk, realise that she was the woman who, next morning, was found battered to death in a South Kensington garage? Who would remember having seen this particular red-head leaving the bar with the new pick-up? What was more likely than that she would take him back with her in the car and that when they got to the garage he, by that time thoroughly drunk, would try to make love to her behind the closed garage doors and she resisting, he would pick up any tool that lay handy and . . . do what he did!

Really, the police were sometimes expected to solve problems impossible of solution. And so great was the burden of responsibility the public put upon them, that they were obliged to pay undue attention to circumstantial evidence.

Furthermore, they were also bound to make much of those small pieces of direct evidence . . . one fingerprint, for instance. A few reddish hairs.

It would be left to the defence counsel to point out that there were no blood-stained clothes found in the possession of the accused, no blood-marked shoes; those facts might have an effect on the mind of the jury, but a man arrested is already half-way to being guilty, she thought.

And as for there being no motive, she knew, with sadness, that at least half of the convicted murderers appear to have no motive for the crime; motive was the most paltry and ultimately unimportant circumstance in what was known as the greatest crime of all.

Time was passing slowly. There was more activity now in the flats. Children, now more tidily dressed, were being taken out in the car with their parents to visit their grandparents; old people were taking a stroll in the warm sunshine; young parents were wheeling out the new baby in the super new pram; some husbands were going off to golf; some young couples to play tennis.

Miss Brown's head was nodding and, each time it happened, she jerked it back. Smilingly now, she was remembering her father's advice to murderers, as he laughingly called it: " always leave the weapon on the spot " and, when the young Hermione had asked why, he had told her that it invariably made things more difficult for the police: "but remember to wipe off the fingerprints!" And, incidentally, she remembered, his second golden rule had been: "And don't talk." But they invariably did; often they kept quiet up to a certain point but, beyond that point, nine out of ten murderers let go, lost control of their tongues and talked and talked and talked . . .

She slept, though afterwards she would never admit it to anyone but herself. She slept.

In the meantime, in the flat overlooking the car, Mr. Charlie Cross, ever the opportunist, had had a previously-booked telephone call to his now convalescing friend, Perce, who, with his wife, was combining business with pleasure at a jazzy little hotel near Le Havre. He then telephoned to certain business acquaintances, rang up British Railways Southern Section, put a few personal requirements into a zip-fastened canvas grip, kissed plentifully the woman-with-whom-he-was-living whilst patting her on the behind and telling her it was all in the day's work, put on his camel hair coat, tied the sash briskly and neatly, put on a hat which he rarely wore, reluctantly took his gloves from the woman-with-whom-he-was-living, kissed her again, went out of the flat, closing the door behind him, descended the stairs and crossed over to his car where Miss Brown was now candidly asleep, her head against the back of the seat and looking pathetically helpless.

Looking at her through the window, Charlie said a very rude word indeed, adding: "you interfering old . . . ing bitch!" and hurried away with his curiously pigeon-toed gait and exaggerated shoulders, to catch the five p.m. from Victoria, watched from the window by the woman-with-whom-he-was-living, who loved him.

And even the harsh words with which he went out of her life were not to wake Hermione Brown; her head slipped a little farther sideways and her mouth fell a little more widely open.

. . . which goes to show, she was thinking as she woke up, *that women of my type are out of touch with reality; even in a matter of life and death, we must have our Sunday afternoon nap.* Her mouth

was dry; she brushed imaginary pieces of fluff from the lap of her skirt, hurriedly pulled the lapels of her jacket together as though guilty of slightly indecent exposure, patted her hair and suddenly became aware that she had been wakened by a tapping on the window beside her and that she was being stared at.

Miss Brown put everybody with dyed blonde hair into one category: tart. The tart now opened the door of the car and said: " Did you want anything? " She was wearing a smart black and white checked suit, with a crocodile handbag and a tiny beret perched jauntily on her blonde hair. She was holding black gloves and was clearly on her way.

" I'm waiting to speak to the owner of this car."

" If you mean Mr. Charlie Cross, it's not his car."

Missing the faint accentuation of the pronoun, Miss Brown looked annoyed; in fact, if it had not been for a certain sleepiness still with her, it might be said that she had glared. " I know it is his car."

With patient forbearance, the blonde returned that it was not his car but belonged to a business friend of Mr. Cross.

" A quibble," Miss Brown snapped back.

" Mr. Cross has been called away on business," the blonde seemed to be saying. " He has asked me to garage the car whilst he is away, in his friend's garage in Finchley. So that is where I am going now, if you wouldn't mind——"

Miss Brown was, for the moment, incapable of moving. She felt firstly an overpowering weakness and secondly a great anger with herself and lastly a feeling of such bitter frustration and futility that there was a hot stinging behind her eyes which she had not felt since she was about nine years old.

The blonde was kind; she sensed at once the distress she had caused. " Come up and let me make you a cup of coffee," she suggested.

Slowly and wearily, Miss Brown got out of the car, crumpling up the paper bag which had contained her picnic lunch and looked round for a litter bin. " Never mind that, give it here. Come on upstairs, you looked fagged out."

For the first time in her life, Miss Brown felt she was really climbing the stairs, as people in books did, climbing as opposed

to simply going up. As the blonde fumbled in her handbag
for her keys and was opening the door of the flat, she noticed
the charm bracelet on her wrist, hung with a variety of
fascinating tiny gilt ornaments. She noticed the slim ankles
and the three-inch heels.

The kitchenette, surprisingly, was scrupulously neat and
clean with shining formica tops and stainless-steel that was
almost dazzling. She flopped on to a stool of which there was
one on either side of a small table against the wall

With rapid movements, the blonde prepared two cups of
coffee, then sat down, putting a bowl of brown sugar between
them and saying: " Help yourself." Almost immediately she
jumped up and brought a bottle of rum out of a cupboard.

" I hate it," Miss Brown said rebelliously.

The blonde poured the spirit into Miss Brown's coffee and
her own liberally. " Never mind, you need it," she sipped the
coffee appreciatively, " and so do I, come to that."

They sipped their coffee in a sudden atmosphere of com-
panionship. And presently Miss Brown said: " What a very
pretty bracelet."

The blonde fingered the starboard light, a pig, a telephone,
the Eiffel Tower, a rocking-chair, a bottle, a horse and jockey,
all in miniature.

" Yes, isn't it? " She toyed with her baubles thoughtfully.
" It was Charlie's idea. He gives me one every occasion,
like."

" I see. It isn't one given by every lover, then? "

The blonde looked up sharply but Miss Brown had said
it with a smile and without a trace of malice; she said it as
one who had read about such things in novels and was amused
and interested.

" No," the blonde shook her head slowly. " I've never had
but one. I guess it's the colour of my hair that made you say
that." And then she said the strangest thing, strange in that it
was said so early in their association; Miss Brown had never
met anyone who talked of anything but the merest formalities,
the weather mostly, within the first steps of acquaintanceship.

" I've got to do meself up like a tart," she said astonishingly,
" they like it; makes them feel big when other men turn to

look. When your face isn't all that smashing you've got to look smart. He's a lot younger than me, you can see that at a glance."

She refilled their cups with both coffee and rum and sitting down again and cupping her face in her hands, she looked across the table at Miss Brown. " I did ought to wear glasses, so I grope around, hoping I won't get run over. If you don't mind my saying so, dear, you'd look a lot younger without those huge great glasses. Your skin's a lot younger-looking than mine. You remind me of that Hepburn girl in the film *Funny Face*. Do you remember, when she worked in the left wing bookshop? All glasses and straight jumpers and low-heeled shoes. And then . . . when she was showing off Balmain's clothes . . . yes, you're quite like her! "

Miss Brown could think of nothing to say. She sipped her coffee with great enjoyment, feeling much, much better.

On she chattered and, as she talked, Miss Brown listened, feeling more and more relaxed, happy even. She talked about Charlie's likes and dislikes, about his moods, the way he would want to go " up West " to a night club one night and sit at home listening to jazz on the wireless at other times. How she liked rum and Charlie liked gin, how she tried liking gin to keep up with him, how Charlie never got drunk but how he did like a double gin and sherry. How he didn't care much about his food but how she was educating him about food the same way he was trying to educate her about drink. And so on.

Thinking it over afterwards, Miss Brown realised that it was all a wonderful exposition of practical psychiatry. The blonde asked no questions, though the air had crackled with them. She treated Miss Brown with the easy familiarity of someone who had been on friendly terms with her for years so that Miss Brown had neither the opportunity nor the desire to ask the many questions that had been burning the tip of her tongue.

So when the blonde had talked and talked and talked it would have been ungracious of Miss Brown not to take her turn. When it came, she accepted a cigarette and began: " I really wouldn't have troubled you, I feel so . . . so importunate but this man Leslie Dunright, the business friend of your—of Mr. Cross—as you probably know, has been arrested for murder. Isn't it a terrible thing!" The blonde was nodding her head understandingly. "Once you're arrested you're already half-way to being found guilty. I feel I must help him because he's so completely alone. Except for Mr. Cross——" It all came out, down to the kittens and the broken window sash. Everything.

The blonde listened attentively, nodding from time to time. Once she snatched off her beret and threw it casually on to the dresser, ruffling her dull butter-coloured hair.

In a few neat phrases, Miss Brown found herself describing Elizabeth Lyneaux in brilliant pastiche undoubtedly inspired by the rum.

"But he couldn't have killed her."

The blonde cleared her throat, not having spoken for a long time: "Why not?"

"Because . . . when she was found the next morning, she had been dead at least eighteen hours. I asked the police inspector to be quite sure about that, when I was being interrogated. Rigor mortis had set in, if you know what that means?"

Flinching a little, the blonde admitted that she did know what it meant. "But there is always room for mistake, they say, by an hour or so. As I see it, there's not a lot in it. Leslie could have met the Lyneaux woman that evening on his way back to the hotel; she might have given him a lift and he gone to the garage with her to put the car away before going back to the hotel. There's lots of possibilities."

"I agree it wouldn't settle the matter altogether but, if your . . . if Mr. Cross would come forward and say he was with Leslie until seven-thirty, it would do a lot to make the police think again."

There was a long pause.

"Absolutely nothing else can save him; I'm sure of it," Miss Brown went on at last. "He's lost all hope, all desire to fight. He doesn't care now whether he's convicted or not. He's not going to lift a finger to save himself."

"What makes you so dead certain he didn't do it?"

Miss Brown thought carefully. The rum made her feel able

to sort out her thoughts with splendid accuracy, rejecting the worthless and extracting the good.

"There are no facts that tell me for certain he didn't," she answered at last.

"You simply feel sure he didn't, is that it?"

"Yes," she nodded, "that is it."

The blonde inhaled and exhaled a long thin stream of smoke in the way women of her kind do when they are feeling women-of-the-world and about to say something profound. But there was nothing phoney about her other than her appearance.

"People are always a surprise," she said, "you never know, do you?"

"How do you mean?"

"Take that sex murderer Heath; everyone who ever met him thought him ever such a charming young man. And there was Haigh who lived in a hotel in South Kensington and all the old ladies doted on him, so much so that they confided their money affairs to him! And even that ghastly Christie, with all those dead women crammed, simply jammed into his scullery like sardines—look how he charmed one girl after another who came to see the flat he had to let!"

"You can't mention Leslie Dunright with all those villains! I mean, you've only got to meet him and you'd know for certain he hadn't done it."

"Leslie Dunright or Leslie Williams," the blonde said slowly.

Miss Brown quickly lowered her eyes to her cup of coffee because now there was a touch of bitterness in her tone.

"Leslie Williams," the blonde went on and what she had to say was comparable to a dentist's drill which occasionally touches the nerve with agonising effect: "Leslie Williams, the mother's boy, butter wouldn't melt in his mouth. For years and years the trusted employee of a famous bank. Meek and mild, gentle as a little child——" she stopped as she stubbed out her cigarette.

"Want me to go on?"

Miss Brown nodded, she could not speak.

"And all the time, building up inside himself, was the

longing to be something better than what he was. To cut a dash. I daresay there is a proper medical name for it. And then one day, a day no different to any other, he tears everything up . . . woops, like this," she made violent tearing motions which were more descriptive than words. " Woops, woops, woops! . . . everything overboard! All the trust, all the friendship, all the love——"

She snatched her handbag and brought out a minute handkerchief, wiping her eyes and blowing her nose. " Hark at me; I did ought to be in the B.B.C. drama rep. Never thought I had it in me. Want me to go on? "

Miss Brown nodded.

" You won't like it."

" Go on please."

" He takes a hundred pounds in fivers out of the bank till at lunch time and walks out of the bank with it in his pocket, just like that. Walks out like he was going out to lunch, same as every day but, instead of that, he goes to his home where he knows there'll be nobody there. He's left a bag packed all ready the night before with his best suit, new shoes; he's had it planned for weeks, months; he's off to Paris to start a new life under a new name; hotel room booked, air ticket bought, reservation fixed . . . the lot! "

They stared at one another across the small table, searching each other's faces and at last Miss Brown used her voice which came out quite cracked and old.

" Not the lot . . . not murder," she said, " because you're his wife, Lil! And you're alive! " she added, astonished.

CHAPTER VII

A LETTER posted that Sunday evening to the governor of the remand prison, a personal telephone call from his secretary to Hermione Brown at the library on Monday morning, and she was given leave from the library on Monday afternoon to attend to urgent private affairs. This time she was allowed to see the prisoner in a small office alone. She had asked for this concession but, when he came in, the warder closing the door but staying, presumably, immediately outside, she jumped up in some confusion.

For the first few minutes they talked of his personal welfare; laundry, food, fruit, newspapers. His manner was dull and impersonal, as though he did not care in the least what he ate or drank or wore. It went on much longer than Miss Brown wanted but she could not break the barrier of formality between them. It was left to him.

" What have you come for," he asked dully, at last.

She had been awake most of the night, sitting in the armchair in her bedroom, nursing her kitten and wording and re-wording what she was going to say to him. She had intended to hold forth at some length, to lead up gently and firmly to the climax of what she had to say. By getting-up time, she had got it more or less word-perfect but now she abandoned it completely.

He had lost some weight, his hair had been ruthlessly cut so that his neck looked miserably thin and the collar of his shirt nowhere touched his neck.

More than ever she found it impossible to believe that this man could raise such a tornado of anger that he could slay with repeated blows anything, any living thing, let alone someone whom she believed he had loved, after his fashion.

She covered one of his hands with her own to soften what she was about to say. " You see, Leslie, you have no belief in yourself so how can any of us have any belief in you? This counsel you have doesn't seem to have a great deal of interest in your case. But can you blame him? I don't suppose he is particularly intrigued; defending you is a mere formality."

"Well?"

"If you had any money we could find a barrister who would really show some interest. My solicitor brother now runs my father's business, quite a well-thought-of firm in Gray's Inn. I can get his advice and he, I am sure, could get some young ambitious counsel to take up your case for a reasonably small fee. Any young barrister whose speciality is crime would jump at the chance to defend you, but they simply can't afford to do it for nothing."

"I have no money, other than the fifty to sixty pounds I was going to spend in France on our holiday——" He looked away quickly. "And that is going on my day-to-day expenditure. It will have to last me until I'm a permanent guest of Her Majesty . . . or hanged."

She pushed her glasses up over the bridge of her nose. "No money at all?"

"No."

There was a long pause. She changed the subject.

"I don't think you realise quite how serious this is. Are you, by any pathetic chance, still hoping Charlie Cross is going to come forward to clear you?"

No answer.

"Because he's not, you know." She took off her glasses and rubbed them vigorously with her handkerchief. "Don't ask me how but I've 'tracked him down' as one might say."

He looked up quickly. "You have?"

"Yes, but——"

"He'll do nothing for me?"

"It's not that. We've been attaching too much importance to what Charlie Cross can do for you. All he can do is to say you were with him till seven-thirty."

"That's right. And Elizabeth died during the afternoon."

She clicked her tongue impatiently. "About eighteen to twenty-four hours dead, they said, and that leaves quite a big margin for error. It doesn't take long to murder somebody. The Birmingham murderer killed a girl and cut off her head with an ordinary dessert knife, all in about twenty minutes."

"Oh, for God's sake!"

But she continued calmly: "One blow, if it has enough strength behind it, can kill a woman. And how long does one blow take? Poor Elizabeth had lots of blows. She may not have died at once. They cannot tell exactly whether she did or not. She may have been unconscious, with her blood still circulating, for an hour or so before she died. No, my poor dear Leslie, we've both been attaching too much importance to Charlie Cross and what he had to tell. And I'm afraid Charlie has put himself out of harm's way. He's gone to France!"

"Oh, my God!"

"Yes," she went on dryly, "Charlie belongs to a highly organised smuggling group or team or whatever you like to call it. Don't ask me how they function, I don't know, and I don't want to know. But one thing I do know is they're not going to get caught."

"I should never have agreed to sell anything that was smuggled into the country. He said he had a licence!"

"Don't sound so smug!" she told him sharply. ("A regular whited sepulchre," she added to herself.)

"I should say those things you sold in the market were all right; he liked to be known as a 'regular trader.' But he has a friend Perce somebody . . . I gather that the business was run in his name, not that of Charlie Cross."

"Don't I know it! Perce-with-the-heart-attack."

"Perce is better now," Miss Brown continued smoothly, "he is out of hospital and convalescing abroad. But it was while he was in hospital that your services were urgently required. Charlie had to have someone he could trust, more or less."

"He picked me up outside a labour exchange."

"Oh no, he didn't," she shook her head slowly from side to side, closing her eyes to show how utterly far he was from the truth. "Charlie Cross was a friend of your wife, Lil."

A whole minute must have crawled by. The clock over the chimney piece above the empty grate seemed to be marking time, like a metronome, until the moment when the whole melody should be worked out. There had to be a succession of parallels before harmony could be attained and she could almost see these working themselves into order in his mind, as they had done in her own.

"Her lover?"

"Yes." She looked down at her still, gloved hands.

He nodded. "It was those damn' twin beds that did it," he said ambiguously, "I said so at the time."

"Perhaps."

"But how long——?"

"I don't know."

"Then why did she go on being, well, kind, shall we say?"

"To you?"

"Yes, to me."

"She was your wife. Wives are unfaithful sometimes, you know. Don't say 'adultress,' Leslie, please, I couldn't stand it."

He ran his hands over his face.

"I suppose you think it couldn't happen to you? Well, it did."

"Then it was Charlie murdered Lil!" he said, surprisingly.

"Nothing of the sort!" she snapped.

"Suicide, then?"

"Not that either. No one murdered her! She wasn't dead!"

The shock of the news seemed to deflate him even further. He kept repeating: "Oh, my God! Oh, my God!" and rubbing his face. Giving him a moment before continuing, she pressed on:

"You drove her nearly off her head, but she wasn't dead! You only thought she was, because you had such a *damn'* guilty conscience!" Her eyes did the nearest thing to flashing that they had ever done and her colleagues at the library would have been astonished as the words poured from her. "Right out of the blue, you wake her up with an early morning cup of tea and proceed to smash up her whole life, tear it up is perhaps the better word. Rip it up in a few minutes. All the years you had spent together, happy enough, at least as happy as those of the majority of married couples, torn up. Can't you understand the shock it was to her? Much, much more of a shock to Lil than you have had just now when you learn she had a lover."

"Oh, I don't know about that."

Miss Brown took off her gloves, resettled her glasses, patted the back of her hair. "Try and see it from her point of view. Lil is about the same age as you. Forty has rushed up on her; as I see it she wanted a chance, probably her last chance, to prove that she was a woman still attractive to men. You never told her she was attractive, did you?"

He was staring at her fixedly and did not answer.

"Did you? You never noticed her, so busy planning your own fine future you didn't even see her around. Charlie Cross came into her coffee bar one afternoon, when there were few customers, and they got talking. He came again, and again, and again. Lil is the motherly type . . . you may not agree, but she is a wasted mother and young men like Charlie are often attracted by women quite a lot older than themselves. So it drifted into an affair and Charlie often used to go back to the flat in Ealing with her when she was off in the afternoons." She cleared her throat and added smoothly, "They used to set the alarm clock so that he would be well away after a cup of tea, before you got home."

He was shocked, his face showed it only too plainly.

"You wouldn't be in the least shocked if you heard it had happened to any other couple."

"I would!"

"Well, you shouldn't be," she snapped. "They weren't doing any harm to anyone."

"I don't know about that!"

"Anyway, no more harm than you were doing to her in your planning to leave her."

She had won that point, he simply murmured, "I thought I'd seen him before. I must have seen him walking away from the flats on my way home. I thought I'd seen him before!"

"Possibly. Charlie is unmarried and, as I see it, Lil is merely an episode in his life. Lil is, as she puts it, 'crazy about him' but she's not so foolish as to believe it will last. Being crazy about someone and loving someone are two different things. She loves you."

He made a disbelieving sound.

"If she did not love you, she would have been overjoyed to hear that you were walking out and leaving her 'to get on with it.' But instead of that, what did she do? She cried so much that she couldn't possibly go to work. Her eyes were swollen so that she could hardly open them. She telephoned to the coffee bar to say she was unwell and then she was going to telephone to her relatives but she didn't. She wandered about the flat in her nightdress, nearly frantic with misery. She looked for and found your suitcase in the cupboard, all ready packed——" Miss Brown paused for words. "She was literally distraught. But instead of rushing to the bank to make a scene or round to the neighbours or any other thing of the kind, she did what I would have done. She decided to go back to bed, and she took four of those sleeping tablets she has had by her for years to make certain she would sleep. Only four, but she was unused to them. Shortly after one o'clock, she woke up vomiting, and was violently sick. She tried to get up to go to the telephone because she knew Charlie would be asking for her at the coffee bar and she wanted someone to give him the message that she was not well, but she couldn't stand up; she broke out into a cold sweat and, feeling for her own pulse, she couldn't even find it! They must have been horribly strong, those pink tablets!"

He was now sitting with his knees apart, elbows on knees, his head buried in his hands. Miss Brown looked at him compassionately.

"You must try to understand how she felt, not how you felt, how *she* felt. If you had waited until evening before coming home, she would have recovered; she would even have been strong enough to face you; as it was you arrived right in the middle of her crisis. She lay there, hardly breathing, hoping you might possibly not come into the bedroom. All sorts of things flashed through her mind in that minute or two. You might have come back to say you were sorry, but you couldn't have done that because you would know she would be away. She might beg you to stay, now that you were back. But above all, she felt pride, Leslie, pride. Do you understand? She could not let you see that what you had said to her that early morning had hurt her so terribly. Do you understand?"

Without looking up he shook his head. "No."

"When you came in, she simply lay absolutely still, as she was, over the side of the bed, as though asleep."

"Pretending to be dead?"

"You're quite wrong. She simply pretended to be asleep because she did not know how otherwise to behave. She was still feeling frightfully ill, remember. You thought she was dead because you were in a panic."

"I pulled her back on to the pillow and tested her breathing with a mirror!"

"You did? If the room's reasonably warm the mirror is warm too; it only works when the mirror is quite cold!"

There was a long pause.

"Why didn't you go to France?" she asked. "Was that panic, too?"

"I couldn't," he whispered, so that she had difficulty in hearing.

"Why not?"

"I still had my passport, Leslie Williams."

"Oh yes, of course."

"I would have been tracked easily, taking the reservation in my own name."

"Yes, Lil was capable of thought to that extent. Charlie rang up; he had been to the coffee bar during the morning; they told him Lil was not well and he telephoned the flat."

"Yes, the phone rang whilst I was there."

"He got no answer. But where do you think he was?"

Wordless he shook his head.

"At a small café round the corner. On hearing that Lil was ill, he set off at once for Ealing in his awful blue car. But, by pre-arranged plan, as always, he rang up from a nearby café before approaching the flat, making sure she would be there, and alone. There was no reply. He started to walk round to the flat at once, and, my dear Leslie, he passed you on the way to the station, carrying your luggage, your raincoat over your arm . . . whistling under your breath."

She felt like saying " laugh that off " but he was so crushed that she thought better of it.

" You see, they were every bit as good at planning and organising as you. Charlie never went to the flat without ringing first, and he never drove the car into the drive. He used to leave it round the corner, outside that little, well, you can hardly call it a restaurant, a café, let's say, and it was from there he always rang up. There were times he took Lil out at the week-end, for a run to Richmond, or something of the kind, when you were at home. Then Lil would meet him at that little café round the corner and they would go off together."

She looked closely at him. " Do you want to hear the rest ? "

" Go on."

" He ran up the steps to the flat, two at a time and tried the door of the flat. He had no key of his own——"

" Why should he ? " he snapped.

" No key of his own. He rang, tapped, looked through the letter box. Lil heard the noise, but felt much too ill to struggle out of bed, she simply lay, as she was, pulled back from the side of the bed on to the pillow by you. One can only guess at what was in Charlie's mind when he saw you walking away with a suitcase, the flat door locked and no answer to his ring. He was off after you like a greyhound after a hare and the train in which you were sitting had not moved out of the station when he got there." She was folding and unfolding her gloves. " Charlie knew you well by sight and yet you didn't know him. You don't notice people much, do you ? Or was it that you were so full of your own affairs ? "

" Oh, I knew him vaguely. He was familiar, only I couldn't think where I'd seen him before."

" I must say this for Charlie Cross, he's a bright lad. He doesn't waste time, he acts on the spur of the moment; he's a kind of spring-heeled Jack," she said with feeling. " He'd taken a ticket to the far end of the line and there he sat in the train, watching you, and when you got out, he got out; when you changed trains he changed trains; when you got to Cromwell Road he followed you down the road to the air terminus;

he watched you. He followed you to the wash-room, waiting outside till you came out; he sat at the other end of the waiting hall watching you waiting. He saw you walk to the litter bin with your tickets, he saw you startled by an official, he saw you put the air tickets back in your pocket. He went on watching till you decided to stay, not to go on your air trip. He followed you along the Cromwell Road as you went in and out of numerous hotels, trying for a room. Finally he saw you going into the Lugano, and there you stayed."

" Fantastic! "

" Not at all. We've all got murder pretty near our surface consciousness these days; any of us may be murdered anytime. He thought that you had murdered Lil, having found out that she was unfaithful to you. What could be more natural than that he should follow you? If Lil had been murdered, he would have been heavily involved. People like Charlie Cross are frightened of murder; they'll take all sorts of precautions to avoid being . . . suspected. No, it wasn't in the very least fantastic. Lil has explained everything to me."

" And what then? "

" He went back to the flat and forced the door open, with his shoulder and the help of a metal nail file for the Yale lock. He's a very strong young man, that one. And found Lil alive and shocked awake by the noise at the flat door. I think we can leave the rest to imagination; Charlie spent as much time with her as he could . . . let's leave it at that. In a day or so Lil went back to her work."

" But there was something else———"

Miss Brown was now doing nothing short of mauling her gloves. " There was . . . I was coming to that. The bank———"

And now he raised a haggard face and looked directly at her.

" Don't worry," she said calmly, " I understand perfectly about how you came to steal that hundred pounds. It's all in the books on psychology that I have read. I won't go into that now, but there is a name for what you did. You followed a certain behaviour-pattern. For everything to be completely in accordance with that pattern, you should have sent the money back by now." She paused. " Did you? "

"Why didn't I hear anything more?" he countered. "Why wasn't there a hue and cry out for me?"

"Because you had been their trusted employee for many years. Absolutely reliable and trustworthy, they understood that you were suffering from overstrain . . . a nervous breakdown."

"You mean they did nothing?"

"Other than send someone, whom Lil describes as 'such a nice, kind, understanding person' to have a talk with her."

"So that was how it was; and all the worry I've had!"

"And what about Lil's worry? She knew, or rather, she said she was sure you would send the money back otherwise you 'wouldn't have a happy moment.' But then, and you know it all fits in, in the most extraordinary pattern . . . Charlie's friend Perce, how he crops up! . . . he had this coronary thrombosis and had to go to hospital."

"Don't I know it!"

"Which absolutely paralysed Charlie's earning powers. You see, one of them used to go and buy the goods and the other would sell. They have no capital to speak of, it's all done by cash transactions. There is no bank account, and hence no income tax to pay and no records of what sales have taken place. Oh, my heaven!" Miss Brown sighed heavily, "I could hold forth on that subject. I could stand on a packing case in Hyde Park and shriek myself hoarse about the present day highwaymen . . . yes, highwaymen . . . but never mind that now."

"So he was stuck for someone to help him and Lil had the idea I might fill the bill?"

"Just that."

"He's a great little old actor," Leslie observed bitterly, "appearing to be taken aback when he heard I couldn't drive!"

"He was getting a bit desperate; he waited in the car at the end of the street and watched you leaving the hotel once or twice. It was your Lil, who knows you like the back of her own hand, who sent him to the Labour Exchange. She had a small bet with him that you would go there first thing in the morning because you'd go out early from habit, and to the

Labour Exchange because you needed a job and you wouldn't know where else to go. He'd been there several times and had just about given up hope when you did go; that morning you went to the Labour Exchange was a stroke of luck for him. Otherwise he was going to try scraping up a meeting in a pub."

" So Lil was at the back of it all! "

" She was. Your touchstone, Leslie, your talisman! Your lucky star! You can't do without her, you know. She knew you weren't taking any money out of the joint account; she knew you wouldn't touch that, as she puts it, ' with a barge pole.' She knew that apart from your casual pocket money, you'd have nothing to live on other than that hundred pounds, and, as she said, you wouldn't use that either if you could help it. She understands you utterly. You're lucky. Ninety per cent of us have to scrape along in this world without being understood. You . . . not."

" So she arranged for me to get a job, or an occasional job," he muttered unhappily.

" She did. And she made quite sure you were paid about three times what you were due. She's got Charlie Cross weighed up, too. Lil's capacity for understanding seems to be boundless," she said in admiration. " Aren't they allowing us a nice long talk? Now, before they come for you, is there anything else you want to know? "

But not until the last moment, pulling on her gloves in readiness to depart, with the warder fidgeting to show that the interview must really end, did she ask her question:

" And the hundred pounds? Did you send it back? "

" No."

" You blewed it, then? "

He was now chattering away about himself like a child who has been forgiven. It was as though he was telling himself that, of course, he had known all along Lil was not dead and was prepared to discuss indefinitely this strange and fascinating subject that was his self.

" Not that, either. I know I'm stupid but I'm not all that stupid! I've had an odd feeling all along about those fivers. I can hardly explain it except by saying I was superstitious about them. It was almost as though, so long as I didn't use them, I hadn't taken them. Yet I couldn't quite bring myself to send them back, I kept putting it off. Then I was suddenly absolutely sick of them; I got to the state when I could have given them to a beggar or stuck them down between the bars of a drain cover."

" So what did you do with them ? "

" They were what a criminal would call ' hot.' I was to go away with Elizabeth and I got the idea I might get nabbed going through the customs . . . oh, I dunno! I got cold feet about the whole thing! "

" But *what did you do with them ?* "

" I put the lot on a horse. Bookies must get any number of hot notes . . . it seemed the best way. I did it on impulse."

" The whole lot! "

(Oh, wonderful son that can so astonish a mother!)

" The whole lot."

" And lost it ? "

" I suppose so."

" You only suppose so ? "

" Well, I should have heard if I'd won! "

Miss Brown looked so pinched that he added: " You could ask Sawley."

" Sawley! " she said, bewildered. " You mean the hall porter ? "

" The same."

" Oh, well . . . that's it, then." She sounded tired. " I'll say good-bye, Leslie. There doesn't seem to be anything more to be said, does there ? "

Leslie was thinking. " Don't say anything to Sawley. Better not."

" Why on earth should I ? "

" I mean, I'm sure he's honest. If you asked if the horse had won, it might make him think I thought he'd trick me. I don't want to make any more enemies than I need. Of course, he'd have told me, by letter or something, if I'd won. He'd have been as pleased as I would. So let's leave it at that."

" All right——"

" And telling me about Charlie Cross following me as far as

the Lugano has reminded me . . . you'd better look out for that kitten I gave you. Sawley hates cats."

" I know he does."

" But you don't know how much. That day I arrived——"

" Was the day my cat vanished."

" It didn't vanish. It was virtually killed by injuries caused by Sawley's foot, I'm afraid. That was how I came to take a room at the Lugano. The cat literally flashed past my face, nearly hitting me slap on, and Sawley was behind it. He got as much of a shock as I did, and to laugh it off, as it were, he was decent and helpful about my getting a room there."

" You mean . . . he kicked it? "

" Like a cannon ball fired from a gun. He must have broken every bone in its body. It landed in the road and shot off, the way cats will, but only to die behind some dustbin, poor wretch."

The metamorphosis in Miss Brown was hardly less marked than that of Lot's wife; she had nothing more to say, she was tense and rigid with anger and then Leslie seemed suddenly sorry that he had upset her.

" I'm sorry," he muttered, " I shouldn't have told you. Perhaps it was reaction . . . so far to-day you've done all the hurting . . . I suppose I wanted to hurt back."

And then he came forward and took both her hands. " I want you to know how very grateful I am to you for all you have done for me. I don't know why you have been so kind; there seems to be no reason for it except that you're good. I am absolutely worthless, hopeless, mixed-up, misguided, mistaken, misbegotten . . . God, I'm not worth it. Leave me now and let things take their course. I deserve everything I'm going to get. But I want to say thank you and would it be presumptuous to add: bless you? "

It was that sort of thing which made people worth saving.

CHAPTER VIII

She had to get a taxicab home; her mind was so perturbed by her thoughts of people who kicked cats and of the frustrations of bank cashiers that she could hardly have found her way to the right bus stop for the confusing humming in her ears. She hurried out of the prison gates, picking up a cruising taxi at once. As official prison visitors usually have their own cars, the taxi driver guessed that she was a relative and in consequence he drove across London sympathetically, taking no undue risks and keeping at a nice soothing speed.

She was burning with sympathy for bank cashiers, that group of quiet, humble, unambitious people who serve the community faithfully and courteously. On a very moderate fixed salary, they sat all day long in sumptuous surroundings in their shabby second-best suits, civil and patient, never losing their tempers with some of the stupid people with whom they had to deal, always smiling a pleasant " Good morning " or " Good day," patiently adding up uncompleted columns of figures in paying-in books, pointing out mistakes in wrongly filled in cheques, asking for more correct endorsements. Hundreds and hundreds of pounds passed daily through their fingers and yet they never appropriated a single one. In times of stress, sickness of a wife, dire need of a child, illness of some beloved person, when a few extra pounds would have made all the difference, did they ever help themselves to a little of the endless stream of money they handled? Never. Though they may have a trade union, Miss Brown thought grimly, they had never been known to strike.

Was it surprising, then, that one in, perhaps, a few thousands should go adrift as Leslie Williams had done?

He was no petty pilferer; the stealing of the hundred pounds had been to him a gigantic act of anarchy, on as vast a scale as if he had removed the entire contents of a strong room. It was the culmination of years of repression in a closed-in personality. He was not one to make intimate friends with whom he could discuss his situation. The gradual drifting away from his wife, had, perhaps, been strengthened every time he had looked at the bank sheets of their personal account. All their recent luxurious expenditure, the foreign holidays, the kitchen improvements, the plushy additions to Lil's wardrobe: everything had been paid for by her and though he had enjoyed the benefit of this expenditure, deep down he had been wounded in a recurring and deadly way.

Miss Brown burned with an overpowering, if unspecified, need to champion the cause of the bank cashier as a whole and of one bank cashier especially.

But at the same time she was ravaged by another kind of burning, and that was rage against anyone who could raise their hand, in this case their foot, against a cat, in particular her darling little lost one with the broken ear and the odd-coloured eyes. . . .

Miss Brown was the sort of person with whom it is not easy to get on Christian-name terms. Though she had been living for years at the Lugano, the shaking old gentleman had never quite brought himself to call her by her Christian name. The slight formality of her manner precluded the intimacy on first acquaintance and the passage of time merely caused it to become a habit not easily broken.

As she stormed up the steps, having tipped the taxi driver liberally, he was standing in the hall, leaning over Sawley's desk, having what appeared to be an intimate conversation with the hall porter. The front doors were propped open and she came in almost silently.

"As I always say, sir," Sawley was saying, "it's all a matter of breeding. Folk pooh-pooh the little matter of breeding these days but as I always say, it's the same with humans as it is with horses. I'd never put a bean on a horse I didn't know nuthin' about, not a bean. It's blood, blood, blood that counts every time——" and, breaking off his strange chant he happened to look up and catch Miss Brown's eye.

"Blood," he said, once more vaguely. "Blood!" And the fifth time he said it his voice cracked and became slightly shrill. The old shaker looked round.

"Ah, Miss Brown, dear! You're back early. There's a

nasty cold wind rising, I'm told. Brr! I'm afraid our little spell of summer is over, what?"

Miss Brown's hand was at her throat and she was breathing as though she had run all the way from Brixton. The old gentleman eyed her severely. "You shouldn't hurry like that; it doesn't do you any good, hurrying!"

The old shaker seemed to be as permanently fixed to Sawley's desk as though he had been grafted upon it in early youth. She stalked past with her head held high because, the more defeated she felt, the higher she held her head, and it had always been thus.

And with every step she took on the stairs her mind said: "Blood .. left ... right ... blood ... blood ... blood ... blood." She must be going mad. As she knew from the innumerable books she had read and plays she had seen, spinsters of her age frequently went mad. The only comfort was that those who went mad did not know they were mad, so perhaps knowing she was mad, or slightly mad, meant that she was not really mad. After all, mad and fantastic things did happen even though they might never have happened to oneself. If it had now become one's own turn to be involved in such happenings, it was no use wasting time deciding whether or not one were mad; it was better to accept the situation as mad and act accordingly.

They were very lenient with mad people these days, she thought comfortably; were you not, she wondered, even left to sign your own certificate in this brave new world?

With this spark of comfort she lifted aside the net curtain which chastely covered the bottom half of her window and looked out on to the leads. She was obliged to keep the window shut when she was out of her room because she did not trust the chambermaid entirely. Though she professed to be a cat-lover and overlooked the saucer upon the leads, Miss Brown was not sure that she would not report the cat's presence to Sawley if she were to find it in her room. Consequently she kept an envelope with: "*Please keep shut in my absence*" drawing-pinned to the frame.

The little cat was immediately outside. Miss Brown opened the window, and it poured over the low sill. She gathered it up and told it the news. Then she placed it on the folded rug at the foot of her bed and went off to have a bath.

There are those who say a tricky situation should never be tackled upon an empty stomach, others hold an exactly opposite view but Miss Brown's knees, which always became shaky upon the slightest of pretexts, benefited greatly from the dinner which she ate without much enjoyment.

In the lounge, where the coffee tray was left for the residents to help themselves, she filled her cup four times. The numbers in the lounge were greatly depleted. One of the old couples had left for the sanctuary of Bournemouth, where they were to recount over and over again their dreadful experiences at the Lugano. The other two couples stayed on, hardly bravely but because there was nowhere else for them to go. And the old shaker stayed out of grim curiosity and interest; like the captain of the foundering ship he would, no doubt, be the last to leave.

Miss Lyneaux, the physicist, Mr. Leslie Dunright . . . . all had gone, for better or for worse. Miss Brown would have liked her coffee to be laced with rum. In fact, never again was she to enjoy coffee as much as she had before the rum episode. The murder was no longer discussed; after the first shock the four old people appeared to have accepted the fact and to be continuing with the business of living their lives with dignity to the end. Coffee was drunk almost in silence and, two by two, they shuffled off to the television room. Miss Brown opened her book and presently the old shaker, who had hovered a while near her, took himself off too.

Would it be Sawley who came for the coffee tray? Or the minion? She did not have long to wait; the old shaker leaving the lounge was the signal that the coffee things were finished with and—praise the Lord!—it was Sawley who came—in his white jacket.

She had not rehearsed anything that she was going to say in her mind beforehand. What she would say would be governed by what he said. With the piping voice of the pseudo-innocent she asked Sawley if he never went out. Oh yes, certainly he went out; didn't she know that by now? After dinner, regular as clockwork, he went round to the

Double Gloucester. Surely everybody knew that? And then there was his week-end, every month, and that was Brighton for him, as a rule. Sawley had received so much praise in his time that he took it for granted that Miss Brown was asking out of sheer admiration for his devotion to duty. She knew, as well as everybody else, that the Lugano could not function without him; therefore her questions were naturally those of one who was pretty idle for one who worked himself to the bone for the benefit of the residents.

" And after lunch? "

" I take a bit of a snooze now and then," he told her, " there's not much goes on of an afternoon." And then he went on to say that he took the opportunity of going along to the bookmaker between lunch and tea, to settle up, as it were. He'd call for his daily paper and buy his fags; he was never out more than an hour.

" And do you usually go in your uniform, Sawley? Or do you change into an ordinary jacket? "

His back was turned to her, he was rattling coffee cups and spoons on the tray and now he was suddenly quiet, and quite still.

Miss Brown felt she had received a blow in the chest which had partially winded her but when she spoke her voice was firm, though still unnaturally high, like that of a B.B.C. *enfant terrible*.

" Because if you were out in an ordinary jacket anyone passing you in the street might not recognise you, might they? I mean, I myself might easily pass you without recognition." She gave the most absurd little laugh, adding unconvincingly: " I only wondered because I thought I saw you the other day and, as I was going to say something, I caught up and found it wasn't you."

He had turned round now and was looking down at her as though she were a large black beetle labouring across the lounge floor. " Indeed."

" Do you ever wear that white jacket, Sawley, when you go out for a half hour? "

He rubbed his hand slowly and thoughtfully round the back of his neck. " No," he returned slowly, " I never wears me steward's jackets out of doors. There's times I wears the commissionaire's uniform and times I wears a sports coat, and times I wears a mackintosh. Is there anything else you'd like to know, miss?" It was said with the utmost politeness.

"Yes," she answered bravely, "as a matter of fact, there is."

"Then let me remove the tray first," he said formally but his eyes had gone slate-hard and she was afraid he might be going out to pick up a cosh.

"No, I won't keep you a minute. It's only about that hundred pounds——"

That stopped him as he was about to raise the coffee tray.

"Hundred pounds, miss?"

"Mr. Dunright's hundred pounds."

He was cruelly unprepared. "Look, miss, let me get rid of this coffee tray and then, eh?"

Giving himself time, she thought.

If he had been wearing his sports jacket to go down the street on the afternoon of Elizabeth's death, and if, during the afternoon, it had become soiled in any way, he would have sent it to be cleaned and there was no possible way of finding out if this were so. If, on the other hand, he had been wearing his commissionaire's uniform and that had become soiled during the afternoon, he would also have sent that to be cleaned and have worn his white jacket in the hall. The weather having been, in the main, fine and spring-like, would anyone have noticed that he was wearing it instead of the uniform? Apart from the fact that she was not there on a weekday afternoon, it was extremely unlikely that she would remember whether he was wearing a white jacket at the wrong time or not. That line of thought, therefore, was unprofitable. Perhaps if she didn't think too hard something else would occur to her.

Within five minutes Sawley was back. "And now, miss, that hundred pounds; you were saying——?"

"Not saying exactly, Sawley, asking."

"Asking what, miss?"

"I understand Mr. Dunright gave you a hundred pounds to put on a horse. It sounds absolutely incredible to me."

"And to me too, miss," Sawley agreed amiably. "I was never so astonished in my life. Nothing like it has ever happened in my experience."

"I should think not. What did you do?"

"Do? What could I do? I'd taken one or two small bets for him but he wasn't a real gambler. He did it in the half-joking way your afternoon picnicker on the heath at Ascot will do it, for a lark. So when he came over with a bundle of notes and told me to put it all on the horse I'd been talking to him about, there was only one thought in my head."

"And that was?"

"It was hot . . . stolen."

"You thought that!" she clicked her tongue, shocked.

"We've had this over before," Sawley said patiently, "what I thought about Mr. Dunright. I think I can pride myself on knowing an honest person when I see one."

She was examining her hands as though she had never seen them before. "You were not so very far off the mark, Sawley. Did you, in view of what you suspected, put the lot on that horse, then?"

Of course he didn't; even as the question was formed, the answer was perfectly clear. He had a mind of his own, he was not merely a conveyer of money from client to bookie. But how would he answer? She could not bring herself to look up, for she was kind and sensitive and did not want to witness the acute discomfort she was causing.

Had she looked up, she might have taken more care.

His face had become congested, contorted as with somebody about to become violently and suddenly sick.

She studied the back of her hand: horrors, she was beginning to get an unsightly brown mole! Or perhaps it was not a mole, she licked her finger absently and tried to rub it off.

"I'm only wondering, Sawley," she went on, still without raising her head, "because I have spent the afternoon again with Mr. Dunright, by special permission of the prison governor this time, and there are quite a number of things I am beginning to understand which I found quite incomprehensible before. Mr. Dunright is very concerned about the money he gave to you. He did it on impulse. What?" She looked up at last. "I didn't hear what you said."

But he had said nothing, only made an exclamation and his face looked as though it were about to come to the boil.

"He is very concerned indeed because he, he had to get rid of those notes." Here she coughed a little because the sudden inspiration she had received caught her off her guard and winded her slightly. "You see, Sawley, they were marked."

"They wasn't in sequence," he barked back. "They was old notes."

"Yes but," she moved her hand, vaguely expressive, "they were all marked with a special mark so that they could be instantly recognised by . . . those who marked them."

"Oh, they was, was they?"

"Yes," she had now decided definitely, "they were."

Turning his back he went over to the window, his hands were hanging by his side and she could see them clenched, with thumbs nervously rubbing the first fingers.

"Some people," she told his back, "wouldn't think a hundred pounds very much; to others a hundred pounds in notes is just the difference between misery and happiness. It's all a matter of relativity." Thinking she sounded too precious, she explained: "I mean a matter of what you're used to. Someone on a small fixed income, for instance, would think a hundred pounds a fortune." And then in a very thin humble voice she said: "Mr. Dunright could do with that hundred pounds now; it might make all the difference to his being properly defended."

He swung round on her so violently that she started back.

"What has that got to do with me? It's gone, see? It's gone!"

"Oh well!" She looked down at her hands again. "It was an unlucky day for us all, that day Mr. Dunright came."

"It was that! You try to help folk and what do you get?"

"It wasn't Mr. Dunright who brought the bad luck, Sawley, it was you yourself!"

He was standing over her now, big and towering above

her. She slipped quickly out of her chair and across to the door.

"Me!" he exclaimed.

"Yes, you, Sawley. You acted like a cruel beast! Don't you know you should never, never harm a black cat?"

CHAPTER IX

IT WAS as though she had carelessly brought the roof down on their heads. Over the whole establishment there was now a kind of stifling stillness, the air laden with small particles of dust as after an earthquake, and a frighteningly significant silence prevailed, as though another tremor was expected to complete the devastation.

In the sanctuary of her room, behind the locked door, she washed her hair and dried it with the hand drier, the use of which was strictly against the rules of the hotel, and which she kept locked away with other belongings in what she called her " treasure chest."

After listening to the late radio play, she wondered if she would be able to sleep as she prepared for bed. She tied her hair into a horse's tail and put on her thick blue dressing-gown. But her mind was so active and excited that she could not even settle down to reading.

She had gone desperately far with Sawley. But then, with Elizabeth Lyneaux foully murdered and an innocent man in custody, things were desperate; the usual formal behaviour did not fit the situation. To try Sawley's integrity by the little trick of telling him the notes were marked seemed, in the circumstances, to be merely common sense. If Sawley's behaviour were completely innocent, the information would have had no effect on him. If, as she suspected, he had kept the money for himself, it might cause anything to happen.

If he had banked the money . . . what then? Would it have been absorbed into the bank's cash-in-hand and have been distributed in the ordinary channels?

If he had not banked the money, would he be keeping it safe, like so many people did, in a *bas de laine*, in an empty tea canister under the floor boards in his room, in a plastic sponge bag up the chimney?

Could that hundred pounds possibly have had anything to do with Elizabeth Lyneaux's murder? Think, think, think! She held her head and rocked herself backwards and forwards. Perhaps Elizabeth had met him on her way home that last afternoon of her life, or while she was putting the car away. It might be that she had known about the hundred pounds that Leslie had given him and had asked about it.

Yes, the more she thought about it, the more reasonable an explanation it seemed. After all, Elizabeth had been killed and there had to be a reason for it; that could fit. Elizabeth's garage lay between the hotel and certain shops; it was perfectly likely that Sawley passed it on his way to and from the shops. Perhaps she saw him pass as she closed one half of her garage doors and beckoned him to come inside for a quiet word with her.

She would have asked him about the money, the name of the horse perhaps, the race meeting, the time of the race, and other details and Sawley in a sudden rush of anger and fear would have picked up the tool he saw lying on the floor. There would have been no struggle; she wouldn't have expected an attack, she wouldn't have had time to cry out; with the first blow down she would have gone against the wall, and the other blows had rained down, assuring that she would never speak again.

Miss Brown, hugging herself now because she felt cold, rocked to and fro, to and fro, gently.

He would have wiped the weapon, at least the end he had held, with his pocket handkerchief. Was he blood-stained? There had not been much blood, so possibly not. But it was a warm day, if his jacket had been blood-stained he could have carried it back to the hotel over his arm and from there it would have been sent to a twenty-four-hour cleaners.

And what about the children who had been playing around? Unless Elizabeth had been killed in that quiet half-hour between three-thirty and four o'clock (and it could not be

proved that she had) there had undoubtedly been children in
the near vicinity part of the evening. But the fact that they
had played ball against the closed garage doors did not prove
anything. Whoever had murdered her had done so within a
few minutes and had gone quietly and unobtrusively away,
closing the doors behind him. She could have been lying dead
or dying behind those closed doors as they played ball against
them.

Miss Brown shuddered. So Elizabeth may have died
because of her outspokenness. If Sawley had had a weapon to
hand this evening in the lounge, Hermione Brown might have
ended in exactly the same way.

But what must she do now? Go to the inspector in charge
of the case with her reconstruction of the crime? Yet another
crazy old spinster, he would think, polite yet amused.

It would need so very little to bring Sawley into the picture;
a receipt from a dry cleaners bearing a relevant date; the
tracing back to him of the spending of a five-pound note at
about that time; or perhaps something significant in a re-
search into Sawley's past.

She smiled grimly as she thought that the one thing necessary to convict Sawley would be a repetition of the crime; he
knew that and knowing it, he was not going to incriminate
himself by leaving Miss Brown's body lying on the floor of the
lounge in the Lugano Hotel whilst he went round to the
Double Gloucester for his evening drink.

With the small hairs on her spine standing up, she realised
that, if he had done so, the chances of her being found during
the evening were not so great. The old people in the hotel
moved slowly and their movements were quite predictable.
They all went into the television room after coffee in the
lounge and there they stayed until after the news. By ten-
thirty they were back in their rooms, the place was deserted
and as quiet as the grave. Sawley could have left her lying
there on the floor of the lounge, gone out for his drink, and
returned to plan disposal of her body in comfort, with a good
seven hours before him, until the chambermaid arrived at
seven a.m. With the management away, the top flat empty,
the younger residents gone, no other resident staff in the hotel,

he was as alone as anyone with a body to dispose of is ever likely to want to be.

He could have carried her back to her room, laid her on the bed and gone away, leaving the window wide open so that the police would suspect the murder had been done by one of those cat burglars who are so clever at climbing in up drain pipes to first-floor windows. He could have cleaned up the mess in the lounge, if any, and gone to bed. And in the morning the chambermaid would find her and the alarm would be raised. Even then, she thought, even then the police might not realise it was he!

The little cat was stretching itself, first one back leg and then the other, in readiness for its night out. Not for anything would she deprive it of this natural habit though in her strange, frightened and imaginative state she would have liked it to stay in, this once, for company.

She kissed it, however, and, murmuring a few words of caution, she seized on one cord of the window, holding the cat in the other, and pulled hard.

There was a sickening thud.

This time it was the right-hand weight! Oh, why, why had she not had them both done at the same time? Putting the cat down, she stooped and pulled at the far too wide-apart finger sockets but she knew from experience that to raise the window was impossible. It was all her own fault, though, because the cord was always more likely to go if she pulled one side only. Damn, damn, damn!

She made a little nest of the rug in her arm-chair and placed the cat in it; then, to show that she really meant it, she took off her dressing-gown and jumped into bed, turning the light out and giving every appearance of settling down for the night. But the cat was not to be deceived. First she heard it clawing the cover of the arm-chair, a habit of which she had tried very hard to break it, and then she felt it pacing up and down the room, with tail erect. When she still took no notice, it sprang on to the bed and paced backwards and forwards across her face. She put out an arm and dragged it under the bedclothes and, though it much appreciated this during the afternoon, when darkness had fallen and the moon was up it would not tolerate it for a moment. It struggled as though in the grip of some sinister fate, scratching its benefactor and behaving like a wild, wild thing.

Turning on the light, she remonstrated with it strenuously but she could see from the expression in its eyes that she meant nothing to it at the moment; it wanted to be out and about and off on its wild lone.

If there was one thing in the whole world she did not want to do at the moment, it was to go downstairs. She thought about the bathroom window, straining to see the geography of it with her mind's eye. Or the window of one of the empty rooms? It was no good; she would have to go downstairs, she could not possibly put it out on to an entirely new and dangerous exit route at this time of night. It was now after midnight and Sawley would surely be snoring in his bed, please God.

She got out of bed, put on her glasses, pulled on her dressing-gown, tying the cord as firmly as though it were a *ceinture de chasteté*, picked up the self-centred animal and went downstairs, leaving her bedroom door open and the light on. The hall and landing-lights were put out at half past ten but the small low-power bulbs were left on at strategic points so, though it was dark, she could see where she was.

Since the murder the front door was bolted at night with an enormous bolt, locked with a mortise key and with a Yale lock and, finally, secured with a chain. She undid all these, opened the door slightly and put the cat out. She watched it mince ungratefully across the portico and disappear down the steps. A dog would have looked back with a wag of his tail; a cat not.

She closed the door very gently, locked the mortise, let the Yale latch slip into place noiselessly, pushed the bolt back home as quietly as she could and was slipping the chain back into its groove when she remained quite motionless. There was a sound behind her but she controlled herself admirably and remained quite still with the end of the short brass chain in her hand. With flinching eyelids, she waited for the blow which she was quite sure was coming. When it didn't come, she slipped the chain home, straightened up and looked round.

There was nothing, no one. The hall, with Sawley's desk scrupulously tidy, was as empty as a stage set without the actors and, somehow, as weirdly significant; ill-lit, it seemed to be waiting for the stealthy arrival of the villain. A streak of light from the street lamp-post shone through the incompletely drawn curtains and that was precisely where she expected to see a snarling and metamorphosed hall porter, with murder in his face and a weapon in his hand.

And yet, she thought, given half a chance, she would go down to Sawley's room, examine the contents of his wardrobe to see if she could find a new dry-cleaners' label on one of his suits, or anything else that might be incriminating. If she knew he were out, she thought, she would not hesitate to do so. Did he never stay out late? In the absence of the management, it was his duty to be back for the night, but who was there to see that he was back? Suppose he were out now, she thought, at some West End gambling hell, losing the money Leslie had given him?

Had there really been a sound behind her or had she imagined it? She went across to the desk on shaking legs, insinuated her small self behind it and tried the locked drawer; Sawley's own particular private drawer. What would he put inside that would necessitate keeping it locked? Not having the slightest idea how to start to pick a lock, there was nothing to be done.

At the far end of the hall from the front door, the door at the top of the basement stairs, opening inwards over the stairs, was hooked open as always in warm weather. In the winter a howling draught came up the icy stone stairs and the door was kept shut during the night. Miss Brown went through the doorway and, standing at the top of the basement stairs and leaning forward as far as she could over the handrail, she looked along the tall, narrow and terribly dismal basement passage, now dimly illuminated by the low-power bulb. It was like one of the dungeons in the Château of Chillon, the difference being that the inevitable smell of boiled cabbage mingled with the smell of fungus. As her eyes became more accustomed to the gloom, she saw with a start that the door of Sawley's room was standing half-open. Did he sleep with his door open? Or was he out? Or was he prowling round the house? And if he were prowling round the house, why did he not turn on the lights? Why was he creeping about in the semi-darkness?

If he was out, then he had gone out at this time of night for one thing, and one thing only: to get rid of the notes which he now believed to be marked. If he were prowling round the house in the semi-darkness, it was for another thing: to silence Miss Hermione Brown for ever.

For a minute or so she was completely paralysed with terror; she hung on to the handrail and did not dare to take a breath lest she should be heard; her heart was thumping away like an old donkey engine. She was sure now that somebody was stealthily moving about upstairs. She heard the familiar creak of a board in the corridor. She longed for the sanctuary of her room and, after a further minute had passed, she knew she must make a dash for it even if the enemy stood between them.

As she gathered up her dressing-gown skirt, freeing her ankles for the dash, she might have been ten years old again, playing sardines with her brothers in the dark old house in Highgate, at that wildly exciting moment before the dash for home when terror and boldness combined in an exultation which reached the point of ecstasy. But this time, she reminded herself, there must be no triumphant scream as she reached home.

Holding her skirts, she flew upstairs and down the corridor almost soundlessly, with her hair streaming out behind her. Her bedroom door was now shut and, with the light out inside; she could see no tiny gleam from the key-hole.

So he was inside, waiting for her! And this time, perhaps, it would be strangulation with those enormous, cruel hands of his. Strangulation took less than a minute, was silent, and needed no weapon. Nor blood. And only someone cruel, who could kick a cat across the road, could do it!

Without waiting a single second to think again, or even to think at all, she turned and as quickly and silently flew downstairs. She unhooked the heavy basement door from the wall and let it close as quietly as she could, skimmed down the long steep flight of stone steps and entered Sawley's room with a blaze of light as she switched it on at the door.

After that everything took on the quality of nightmare and, as always in a nightmare, the dreamer screams; she heard herself screaming as Sawley leapt from the bed, a frightening and rather obscene sight, towsled, grey, unshaven, enormous, and terribly angry.

But withal not unmindful of the decencies of life, he stopped to struggle into his dreadful cardigan, which was upside-down and inside-out and back-to-front, giving Miss Brown time to fly upstairs again and, as she reached nearly the top she received a fearful blow on the forehead.

In many of the books Miss Brown read, at this juncture the heroine, or victim, falls into merciful oblivion and that is the end of the chapter. But to her astonishment, as she fell backwards, down the endless steps, experiencing acute pain, thought went with her, not constructive thought but amazement that she could have been attacked from the front when she had expected to be caught by the ankles and attacked from behind.

At last she stopped moving downwards and lay, presumably at the foot of the stairs in the monstrous grip of pain, but still thinking and now it was: This is what it must be like having a baby. And: I mustn't make a sound: this was what her brothers had taught her. And: if I don't move I can just bear it.

And perfectly clearly she heard the quavering voice of the old shaker: " Good God! Sawley, what is going on? "

" Have you all gone mad? " Sawley shouted. " Who shut the stairs door? Why all this fooling about. Why the hell did she come into my room? "

" Oh, what have I done? " she heard the old man wail.

" Done, you've only killed her! Get out of my way whilst I get to the phone, you old fool! "

And then there was nothing but pain, and pain, and pain, so that she could neither hear nor see but only feel. And after a long, long time, years and years, there was a prick in her arm and, through the red hot bars of pain, she heard a strange man's voice saying: " That's for now! "

And Miss Brown said, because she knew it should be said: " Merciful oblivion! "

CHAPTER X

AND SO FOR a long time there was chaos and darkness and non-comprehension; there was terrible headache, dry mouth, sickness, and pain; there was a succession of pretty young faces surmounted by goffered caps, cool hands and many, many pricks which took away the pain. And she was continually being washed from head to foot.

And then, one day, she was lying flat on her back, encased in some kind of plaster jacket and looking up at the white ceiling when it came to her that she was still Hermione Brown and that she was lying in bed in hospital recovering from a broken neck.

There were lots of visitors; brothers, nieces and nephews, friends, colleagues from the library, all kind and anxious and bearing gifts, but all strangely evasive and, when she tried to find out what had happened, they patted her kindly and told her she must not worry about anything, all she had to do was to get better.

Her favourite niece, a round-eyed child of sixteen with the chubby face of a ten-year-old and the strange clothes of a *femme-du-monde*, finding herself alone in the sick-room, approached the bed and hissed: " Darling Aunt, were you really drunk? "

" No, dear, I wasn't drunk."

" What happened then? "

" I'd got myself worked up about something. I don't really know what did happen."

" Well, darling, in the absolutely small hours you went downstairs in the hotel, in your dressing-gown, and for some reason or other you shut that door at the top of the basement stairs, and then you went down and into the hall-porter's room and turned on the light and when he jumped out of bed you flew upstairs——"

" And then? "

" I shouldn't be talking to you about it. They say you've got to be kept calm."

" Go on, dear."

" One of the old men in the hotel had heard noises. He got up and found your bedroom door wide open, so he turned out the light and shut it. Is he a fussy old busy-body? "

" Yes, go on! "

" Then after a bit he heard more noise, he came out again and saw you going downstairs and so he went after you to see what was happening."

" The interfering old fool."

" He says he never sleeps. He went downstairs and, seeing the door to the basement was shut, he was standing in the hall wondering what next, when you screamed and naturally he opened the door to see what was up and you were there at the top, charging up head first! "

Miss Brown would have nodded had she been capable of it, as it was she agreed, saying that the door was very dangerous, opening inwards as it did; there had been accidents in the past and it was for this reason that it was always hooked open during the day.

" So you see, darling, it's all rather puzzling."

" I'm sure it must be, but some day I will tell you more about it and then you'll understand."

All her visitors and yet with not one could she discuss what lay nearest to her: Leslie Williams's predicament and the fate of her little cat!

But it takes quite a long time to recover from a broken neck and, long before she was out of hospital, the manageress of the Lugano Hotel arrived back home from her interrupted honeymoon and in due course came to see Miss Brown.

Sawley had been unduly upset by the whole affair; he had lost his nerve and had sent a wire to intercept the manageress as she sailed home. She had left the ship and her new husband and had flown home from Naples, to save time. It really had been too bad the way everything had gone wrong in her absence. Though Miss Brown brought up the subject of Miss Lyneaux's murder several times, it became quite clear that she did not wish to discuss it; it lay as a dreadful bar sinister across the hotel's escutcheon. To ignore it as much as possible was to minimise it. If the hotel were to become notorious in an unsavoury way, the name would have to be changed, which would be expensive and cause a number of complications.

But Miss Brown was determined not to let her go without telling her anything she wanted to know. As she was leaving she said: " And Leslie Dunright; please tell me what has happened ? "

" Happened ? "

" Yes, happened," Miss Brown repeated impatiently.

" The trial is one day this week; Sawley has been told to stand by; he is to be a witness at the Old Bailey."

Miss Brown gasped. " But he didn't do it! They can't! "

The manageress was pulling on her gloves before going. " Don't tell me you were taken in by that terrible Dunright too! " she exclaimed.

" No, I was certainly not taken in by him. He simply didn't do it, that's all."

" We'll see, dear," the manageress answered comfortably. " The more I hear about that one, the more I think he ought to hang! Now, you're not to worry yourself. All you have to do is to get better."

And because she was being kind and not re-letting her room but allowing her to keep it on at a nominal sum, Miss Brown smiled and thanked her for coming and said no more about things that did not please her.

At least she knew when she was defeated; with a healing broken neck and not a single constructive idea left in her head, Miss Brown could do nothing but lie and look at the ceiling and try the faith which she had heard so much about.

A few days later, in a very small paragraph on the third news page of the paper, she read that Leslie Williams, known as Leslie Dunright, had been convicted of the murder of Miss Elizabeth Lyneaux (39), in a garage in South Kensington and had been imprisoned for life.

And because she could not turn on her side but still had to lie flat on her back in a kind of cage, the great hot tears flooded down her face, and over her temples into her hair and down into her ears, and into her mouth, almost choking her. And the pretty nurse came up and wiped them away saying: "What's wrong, dear? Homesick?"

It was weeks before she was released from the plastic brace which held her neck straight and served up her head like a stemless flower in an old-fashioned vase. During that time she stayed with relatives and then took a holiday in the South of France. In August, when they needed her most, with the rest of the staff on holiday rota, she was again at her desk amongst her friends, the W to Z's.

The first evening she was back at the Lugano, when dinner was over and Sawley should have been on his way to the Double Gloucester, he came to her room, and he was carrying the little cat.

"Here you are, miss," he said, shamed by his own sentimentality. "It's a horrid little thing but, as me old Mum used to say, it takes all sorts to make a world. You love it, eh?"

"Oh, Sawley——" There was an embarrassing hot stinging behind her eyes and all she could say was: "Thank you!"

"You thought I done it, didn't you, miss? Miss Lino, I mean."

Miss Brown nodded.

"I wonder what gave you that idea?"

But she was not to be drawn.

Sawley went on. "When we was waiting outside at the trial at the Old Bailey, I met the wife, Mrs. Williams. Mrs. Leslie Williams, that is. The trial only took the one day but there was an overspill, see, from the trial before. It lasted a day longer than they'd reckoned so we had a day to do nothink but twiddle our thumbs outside the court on a bench in a marble hall. And this Mrs. Williams and me went for our midday meal together. She's a decent sort. And by the way, miss, she wants to see you."

"Lil."

"That's right. I promised I'd let her know when you was back home, back here, that is. So I sent her a postcard to-day. She'll be along by-and-by, I reckon."

But she couldn't let him go without asking about the hundred pounds.

"There's some might think enough had been said re that hundred pounds," Sawley observed darkly.

"It was only that I knew it was all the capital he had. It might possibly have made all the difference to the outcome."

"To the what?"

"To the result of the trial."

"Not it, pardon me, miss. It wouldn't have made a jot of difference because, as I always say, British justice being what it is, the truth came out at the trial. Bless you, the jury wasn't out above half an hour! No. To tell you the truth, miss, I had been hanging on to that hundred pounds for a purpose. But for what purpose I didn't rightly know. But when I got to the Old Bailey and had a chat with that Mrs. Williams I wasn't in two minds."

"You have given it to her."

"That's right. Next day I handed it to her," he said smugly.

"I wonder what made you keep it, Sawley."

"Insting," he explained. "Mind you, I did put one fiver out of it on that horse for him. It lost by half a hoof's length, bad luck!"

"So you made up the money to a hundred again by a fiver out of your own pocket?"

"That's right. Now, miss, please don't let that blasted cat claw up the stuffing off of the arm of your chair, which is what it's done in my room. Get off of it!" Sawley stepped forward and roughly cuffed the cat to the ground.

When Lil came, her hair was as bright as Miss Brown remembered it, her clothes were as striking, her make-up was as heavily applied, but she was a little diminished in a general way; the same Lil but less so.

Miss Brown had gone out at lunch time and bought a slim quarter of Jamaica rum which she was able to slip into her handbag; the thought of Lil was strongly associated with coffee laced with rum and Miss Brown saw to it that coffee was served in her room when Lil came. She was carrying Miss Brown's mackintosh, umbrella and drizzle boots, old friends from her far-distant past.

Lil had already heard Sawley's account of Miss Brown's exertions; whatever she may have thought of them, she made no comment and allowed Miss Brown to tell her everything all over again in her own way. And when it came to an end, Lil still refrained from comment; she was chain-smoking, lighting a fresh cigarette from the stub of the old one and at the end of Miss Brown's story she had reached the end of a cigarette and there was a long significant pause whilst she lighted another, inhaled, blew out the smoke in a long thin stream and inhaled again. The process was certainly effective, giving the impression that she was thinking over what she was going to say carefully, whereas, on the other hand, Miss Brown had poured out her story too quickly, going back to points she had forgotten, getting confused about time, repeating herself.

Lil said her thanks sincerely, quietly and with feeling, adding: " I only wish you'd been right."

" There's been a terrible miscarriage of justice," Miss Brown said breathlessly. " I have talked everything over with my solicitor brother. I understand your solicitor advised against appeal but, in view of what I have told my brother, he agrees with me that——" but her words petered out as she saw Lil, in a haze of smoke, slowly shaking her head.

" He was guilty, you know. When I first heard about the murder of this Elizabeth and read that a Leslie Dunright, whom I knew to be my poor Les, was ' assisting the police ' as they call it . . . my heart sank. I knew he'd done it, and that's why when Charlie and I had talked it over, we realised there was no point in Charlie coming forward and saying he'd left him at seven-thirty in Sloane Square so he couldn't have done it. No point at all! "

" How could you think such a thing of your husband? " Miss Brown asked indignantly. " So kind, so sweet, so helpless——"

" So mixed up, so frustrated, so much the spoilt boy whose

mother had been everything to him, done everything for him, been his prop and anchor, his whole foundation and then had left him high and dry by dying! It's a funny thing about this mother-love," Lil said thoughtfully. " They say too little of it does harm and they say too much of it——"

" Is lethal," Miss Brown suggested.

" I reckon it's as well I'm not a mother," Lil went on, " it puts too much responsibility on you."

" Oh, I do agree! "

They smiled at one another and Lil blew her nose.

" However——" she went on, " it seems now I was waiting all my married life for something like this to happen. And yet he was what you might call the model husband . . . until that morning! Once he told me he was walking out on me, well, then I could believe anything of him. But now he's done the impossible, gone as far as he'll ever go . . . I reckon Leslie'll never go wrong again, not so long as he lives."

Miss Brown leaned forward. " You're going to tell me he confessed everything; but it's common knowledge that confessions don't always mean anything. If he's confessed down to the last detail, I still don't believe it."

Lil sighed and brought out of her handbag a recent passport photograph of her husband, taken for the trip to France in the name of Leslie Dunright. Miss Brown took it from her and stared down at the perky, upright little man, holding himself stiff and straight, his hair receding in great gulfs on either side of his forehead, a tiny wisp of a moustache on his upper lip.

He looked vain and, yes, awfully sure of himself.

" The silly vain little ass," Lil went on, " gave this to his Elizabeth, an extra photograph he didn't need in applying for the passport. Gave it her," Lil repeated with disgust, " and, if hanging were still in force for that kind of murder, that sentimental, cocky little act would have hanged him."

Miss Brown hugged herself as though in pain. " But how ? "

" To cut a long story short——" Lil went on, " I'll tell you just what happened on that last day of Miss Lyneaux's life, shall I? Well, Les said good-bye to her in the morning, as you all know . . . he went off to the market with my Charlie and spent the day selling shoes for him, right? Miss Lyneaux goes to lunch with her aunt at Harrods, says good-bye to the old lady and goes off to her bank to make last-minute arrangements for the trip to France, right? On the way she stops at a bar and has a couple of drinks; nobody came forward to prove this but when she got to the bank she was in a very lively mood indeed, not exactly drunk but, as the bank clerk said, 'certainly been having a good party.' She got her traveller's cheques and so on and then had a pleasant word with the clerk (this was just before closing time, with very few customers in the bank), about the holiday she was taking in France with her fiancé . . . where they were going and so on. And then she took the photograph out of her handbag and showed it to the clerk: ' That's him,' she said, ' Leslie Dunright.' ' Dunright! ' the clerk says, ' that's Leslie Williams of the City and Suburban.' ' Oh, no,' she says, ' you're quite wrong! ' ''

Lil stopped for a moment to take off her shoes: " Oh, my poor feet! " She cast off the high heels and curled up her toes luxuriously. " That's better! Now that was no coincidence, with Fate, as they say, catching up on him in a big way. Leslie's always been keen on tennis; two Saturdays every summer he was off to Wimbledon all day, watching the tennis. It never amused me, I let him go alone, and off he would go, rain, hail or snow."

" Did he play himself? "

" No, he didn't care for trying to do a thing, he always wanted to excel, so he wouldn't play himself, but on a fine afternoon at the week-ends he would go and watch the City and Suburban Bank Tennis Club playing matches at home or elsewhere, has done for years. So it's not very surprising to hear that last summer, when there was a knock-out tournament between the tennis clubs of a group of London banks, Leslie was roped in to do the doings . . . what do you call it? "

" Umpire? "

" That's right. The little sharp chap who sits at the top of a huge tall pair of steps, wears a green eye-shade and acts like God Almighty. Umpire, that's it. Well, this bank clerk of

Miss Lyneaux's is a first-class tennis player and he distinctly remembered Leslie Williams was umpiring a match he was in and he distinctly remembered that he was a City and Suburban man. He told all this to Miss Lyneaux over the bank counter and afterwards, when the police checked up, he said that it had been a bit of a shock to her."

" That's what was behind it all! "

Lil nodded. " This bank cashier was called by the prosecution as a witness at the trial. They'd been trying to get away with it without having to bring other bank employees into it, that's why he wasn't at the first hearing, see ? "

" Well, what happened when Miss Lyneaux left the bank ? "

" What would you have done ? " Lil asked. " This Elizabeth Lyneaux was asking for it, carrying on like that with a man she hardly knew anything about." Lil spoke with the virtue of one who would be very far from doing exactly the same thing.

" Here was this chap called Leslie Dunright she was going away with in a couple of days, and now she was told he wasn't Dunright at all but Williams. It shook her. So what did she do ? She'd got her car with her, battery fixed, everything ready for the trip abroad and a few hours with nothing to do. She got into her car and drove to the head office of the ' City and Suburban.'

" You know what it's like trying to see the right person in a big organisation like that ? She had to wait around for ages but finally she did see an under manager or something of the kind.

" Well, my dear, he was what you'd call discretion itself. He didn't want to say anything but here was a woman in great distress, having discovered that the man she was engaged to and going away with was an ex-employee of theirs under another name ... you should have heard Mr. Discretion Itself in the witness box ! He gave Miss Lyneaux ' certain information ' and I've since learned that he simply told her Leslie Dunright was Leslie Williams who had lately left their employment ' under a cloud.'

" It seems our Les had been boasting to her about a hundred pounds he'd got from the sale of some of his wife's personal property. . . . This Miss Lyneaux was as sharp as a bag of monkeys, wasn't she?"

Miss Brown, remembering the lean little cat's face and the strange green eyes, agreed, though personally she would not have called her intelligence that of a bag of monkeys.

Lil stretched out in the chair, crossed her legs and wiggled her toes in their nylon stockings, now thoroughly relaxed and at home. "No one knows what she did after that. She left the head office shortly before five and it's my guess she went and had tea somewhere; she'd be thirsty after the drinks she'd had. A café somewhere in London town . . . and while she drank her tea, she'd be thinking it all over; what would she do? She wasn't cheerful any more and I guess she was feeling like hell. She'd been looking forward to the holiday with this new little lover like anything and now either it was going to fall through or—not. So what? So she drove back towards the Lugano. As I see it, nobody knows exactly what she did with that two and a half hours, but as Leslie was walking back from Sloane Square, where he'd been sick as a dog after the drink Charlie had given him, she passed him, in Cromwell Road, saw him, stopped and gave him a lift back to her garage."

"I see it all now," Miss Brown said, as though she, too, were going to be sick.

"Les wasn't called by the defence," Lil went on, "he didn't go into the witness box, but he's told me everything since."

"He has!"

Lil nodded. "Poor old Les! That woman was a lot too much for him, wasn't she? How ever did he come to fall in love with that kind? An usherette would have done him all right."

"But what did he tell you?"

"Well, when she picked him up and drove back slowly towards the hotel she told him she'd shown his photograph to her bank cashier and he'd been recognised as Leslie Williams who had been a tennis umpire last summer, and so on. Then she went on to say she'd a pretty good idea why he was masquerading as someone else . . . it was the hundred pounds he'd been talking about, supposed to be from his late wife, wasn't it? Poor old Les was struck dumb, he just couldn't utter a word. You mustn't forget what was far more important than the hundred pounds was the thought of me . . . dead, as he thought, and what he was really worrying about was did she know about me?

"All the way back to the garage she went on. I must say, if it wasn't all so tragic, it does a man good to know that it's not only wives can nag . . . mistresses can too, and in this case. . . . Well, anyway——" She sniffed expressively.

"You mustn't forget old Les had a bad hangover. He'd sicked up most of the alcohol but he had not yet had any food; he wasn't feeling himself, not by a long way. When they got to the garage he got out and opened the doors. She drove in. He bolted the first door whilst she tidied up, picking up the tool kit and letting down the boot. All the time she was talking and he'd said nothing at all, not a word. Then she looked up and said something like: 'Well, damn you, what are you going to do about it?' And that tore it!"

There was a long pause. Lil's throat was working, her voice seemed to have left her but at last she went on. "It wasn't anger. It wasn't cruelty. It wasn't murderous intent, as the judge mentioned, it wasn't . . . oh hell! It wasn't anything but the spoilt boy, peevishly smashing up what he'd so badly wanted but now couldn't have. The spoilt boy of thirty-nine, not nine!"

"Chagrin," Miss Brown suggested.

"He snatched up the jack which she was putting away and simply hit out wildly and bashed away until the thing he'd so loved and wanted was broken."

"Murder in mortification," Miss Brown put in roundly; she was fond of captions.

"It all took place so quickly, seconds, he says, and then he closed the garage doors and was walking back to the hotel. As he left the garage, a group of playing children ran screaming round the side of the house, nearly colliding with him, and yet not one of them remembered seeing him."

"You mean, not one of them remembered seeing a fierce murderer leaving the scene of the crime, blood-stained and wild," Miss Brown suggested. " They only saw a tired, colourless little man in a dingy suit and his second-best shoes and for a long time he didn't believe he'd done it. Thought it was part of a bad dream he had had! "

" Don't cry," Lil said, blowing her own nose again vigorously. " There's a few details . . . blood, for instance. He wiped the jack clean with his pocket handkerchief and later that same evening he flushed it down the loo. There was some blood on him and blood on his jacket sleeve; later he tore the whole jacket in small bits and put the bits in waste paper bins all over London. He popped the waistcoat and trousers——"

" What? "

" Took them to Uncle Joe's. Pawned them at a pawn shop near the Portobello market, then burnt the pawn ticket with his lighter. He doesn't know why he did all this, it was just something to do, he says."

" And there was no blood on his shirt? "

" No, Les never will wear his shirt sleeves down beneath his coat sleeves, I've nagged him about that till I'm hoarse. This time it served him well, there were no blood marks on his cuffs."

Miss Brown did not remember a single occasion in her life when she had run out of words; even now she had not entirely run out.

" The un-hero," she said sadly.

" What, dear? "

She repeated it but Lil merely drained her cup of now cold coffee: " So that's it."

And later Miss Brown asked what she was going to do. She brightened up and said that Perce, the ubiquitous Perce without a surname, was now back in circulation and he and Charlie were doing very nicely.

" I know I've not got much longer with Charlie," she said sadly, " Charlie likes the cream off the top, and when he's had all he wants off me, he'll be away and marry some glamour kid of sixteen whose Pa's got money, you'll see! The best of every possible world for Mrs. Cross's favourite son, and why not? I'll know when he's through with me, I won't hang on. As I see it, I'm lucky, but I'll still have Les. He and I have a lot to forgive each other."

She looked down at her hands whilst Miss Brown stared at her in something very like delight. " Do you mean that? "

" Of course I do. With luck, Les will be out in ten years and by then I'll pretty well have had it; fifty-two, I'll be, to tell you the honest truth, and he'll be pretty near it; we'll both be lonely, we're going to need each other. And by the way, the ' City and Suburban ' got their money back; Sawley gave it to me at the Old Bailey and I took it back to the bank after the trial was over. I had a long talk with the personnel manager, he's a real good sort. He says Les gave them more than twenty years of fine service and, when he comes out, they'll look after him, that's what he said, look after him! " Lil smiled. " Oh, and there's one more thing I must tell you. At the trial . . . after he'd been found guilty, the judge asked him if there was anything he had to say before sentence was passed on him.

" I'd have given anything to see his face but I was sitting in the seats at the back of that blooming great dock, I could only see his back; standing up very straight, hands hanging by his side, like someone standing for ' God Save the Queen.'

" ' Yes,' says Leslie, starting off loud and firm, ' Yes, my lord,' he says, ' I want to say that I am guilty and that I fully deserve any sentence you may pass on me.' And then it was as though he went to bits; he didn't whine and you could see he wasn't sucking up to his lordship but he sounded like he was broken up. He says: ' I dunno what came over me, I wouldn't have hurt a hair of her head. I loved her! ' For the life of me I can't remember what his lordship said, I was crying me eyes out, but you could see the old gentleman was on Leslie's side. He looked sad, kind of, and when he said ' Imprisonment for life ' Leslie turned round to go down the steps to the cell with the two warders and I could see plain and plain there was tears streaming down his face. And that was it! "

" And by the by," Lil said as she was leaving, " your mack and umbrella! The manager of that little caff round the corner where Charlie and I go for fags got proper worked up. ' There was a little lady here,' he said, ' one Sunday morning,

I don't know what she'd got on her mind but she was asking about the folk living in the flats. Brown, she said her name was, Herminy Brown, and I wasn't to forget it. It was like she thought she was going to get murdered; she looked that scared. Would you know her?'" Lil laughed. "That was you all right, that Sunday. I told him I knew you and he said to give you back the belongings with his compliments! So there they are!"

After she had gone, Miss Brown unlaced and removed her shoes, took off her glasses, picked up her little cat and lay down on her bed. She tucked the little cat comfortably under her chin and gently scratching the top of its head she stared up at the ceiling for a long, long time.

THE END